MW00959206

Enchanter's Glass

SUSAN WHITCHER

Enchanter's Glass

Jane Yolen Books
Harcourt Brace & Company
San Diego New York London

Library of Congress Cataloging-in-Publication Data
Whitcher, Susan.
Enchanter's glass/Susan Whitcher.—1st ed.
p. cm.
"Jane Yolen Books."
Summary: Like Britomart from Spenser's "Faerie Queene,"
thirteen-year-old Phoebe is drawn into a fantastic world where
she is pitted against an enchanter who has trapped
in glass the self-images of people close to her.
ISBN 0-15-201245-1
[1. Self-perception—Fiction. 2. Magic—Fiction.] I. Title.
PZ7.W5774En 1996
[Fic]—dc20 95—43879

Text set in Goudy Village
Designed by Linda Lockowitz
Printed in the United States of America
First edition
A C E F D B

To Martin L.,
the boy with cooties

It vertue had, to shew in perfect sight,
What ever thing was in the world contayned,
Betwixt the lowest earth and heavens hight,
So that it to the looker appertayned;
What ever foe had wrought, or frend had faynd . . .
For thy it round and hollow shapéd was,
Like to the world it selfe, and seemed a world of glas.

—Edmund Spenser, *The Faerie Queene*, III, 2

TABLE OF CONTENTS

I	A Piece of Glass	1
II	Phoebe Van der Clute	9
III	Archimago	16
IV	The Faun	31
V	Sir Paravent	47
VI	Sir Brillohead	62
VII	Staci Boyd	80
VIII	Queen Evergreen	99
IX	Angelina	113
X	Tamás Horvath	135
XI	Lewis Barnes	151
XII	The Lady Knight	169
XIII	A World of Glass	192

CHAPTER I

A Piece of Glass

In swimming be expert, through waters force to pas.
—*The Faerie Queene*, V, 2

PHOEBE VAN DER CLUTE sat in the dark at the top of the stairs and thought about falling off the bridge. Downstairs in the bright, warm kitchen, she could hear her mother's voice. Althea was talking on the phone to somebody.

"I could've died," Phoebe whispered. "I almost drowned." What had happened instead was, she found the piece of glass.

She'd gone to the bridge to wait for the school bus. The homebound bus would cross the bridge on its way to Phoebe's stop, at the top of Steephill Road. If she hid underneath she'd hear it drive over. *That way I'll know it's safe to go home*, she'd thought. Anyway, she was tired of hanging around in the woods. So she'd shouldered her backpack, picked up her clarinet case, and started along the path upstream, toward the bridge.

Beside the path ran the river, shallow and chatty. It raced and gossiped with stones, or looped in and out of tiny pools formed by the roots of a maple or willow. Where the Steephill Road bridge crossed over was the only place the water got deep enough for swimming. Not that you could swim in April. If you jumped in now you'd probably die from the shock.

The woods ended at a short strip of gravel beach by a swimming hole. This was as far as Phoebe could go upriver. Beyond the bridge the land on both sides belonged to Mr. Lewis Barnes, who never let kids play there.

Gravel stones rolled away from her sneakers as she walked toward the bridge. Everything else seemed unnaturally still, as if it had been waiting for Phoebe to step out from the cover of the trees. She knew it was stupid and dangerous to come here, where anybody driving by on Steephill Road might see her. They'd know right away she was supposed to be in school. Or Mr. Barnes might be staring out his front window.

Lewis Barnes ran a little business out of his home, THE BARN MARCHÉ—NEW ENGLAND ANTIQUES AND COLLECTIBLES. What he sold was mostly glass—milk glass, carnival glass, heavy glass paperweights with bubbles trapped forever inside. Especially on wet days, Mr. Barnes would stand by his picture window, watching for leaves that blew onto his lawn. As soon as the rain stopped, he went out to pick them up one by one, using a groundskeeper's stick with a nail on the end. He always wore white patent-leather shoes with gold-tone buckles shaped like little bridle bits.

Phoebe stashed her backpack and the clarinet case in the shadow of the bridge abutment. Above her was a ledge in the concrete where she could perch and hold on to the rusty beams that ran under the road. When the school bus roared overhead it would rattle her bones.

If she sang at the same time, the rattle of her jaw would make the song come out funny. Troll music, that's what she and Staci Boyd used to call it. Only, Staci didn't want to come down to the river much anymore.

"She doesn't want to do *anything* anymore. She looks like a zombie, all that junk she puts on her face."

Phoebe'd been talking to her father two nights ago, hanging over the back of the big dust-colored plush armchair where he sat down to read every evening after supper. More and more often now, Pop fell asleep with the book propped open on his stomach.

He's gotten old, she'd thought, *since he had his stroke.*

"*Everybody's* worse this year," she'd told him. "I mean, all of a sudden all these people that I've known all my life practically—everybody's in a click. Even the boys, they hang around in little bunches. And nobody talks anymore. They just whisper."

"Ah. Hm," said Pop.

From the back of the house came the deep, tender voice of her mother's viola. If Phoebe went down the hall to the bathroom, she would see the line of light shining under the door of the room where Althea played. Whenever Phoebe heard beautiful music, she saw in her mind that line of brightness under the closed door.

Phoebe leaned over the chair into the circle of Pop's lamplight. "Staci told Jennifer Gorton I'm immature. '*Phoebe's gotten to be so immature,*'" she mimicked. "I mean, how can somebody just *get* immature? If they weren't before, I mean. Immature's not a *disease,* is it? It's not *catching.*"

Pop sighed. "Well, my dear, I recollect I almost died of old age when I was about seventeen. But I got over it. No doubt your friend Sandy will, too."

"Staci, Pop. Staci was only just *fourteen* at Christmas."

But Pop had gone back to penciling notes in the margins of his *Journal of English and Germanic Philology.*

The air under the bridge felt chill and dank. Phoebe didn't want to hide under there. She was sick of hiding. She wanted to walk out over the bridge, in the sunshine.

She watched her feet carry her up the graveled bank onto the tarred road, as if they'd made the decision by themselves. She turned her back to Mr. Barnes's store and leaned against the bridge rail.

There was a game she liked to play, that the bridge was actually a boat. The boat was flying over the water, taking her to someplace far away and new. The deep water slipped black-green from under the shadow of the bridge. In the sunlight it changed to a trail of bright reflections. She flicked a chip of paint off the parched wooden railing and watched it spin away on the stream. She wanted to go someplace far away and new.

But she couldn't shake off the feeling that there was someone staring at her back. She had to hold on hard to the rail to keep from squirming her shoulders. She leaned out farther and farther, weighed down by a sudden strange despair—as if she'd been pinned to the spot while her personality leaked away through the pinholes. She'd felt like that at school sometimes, when she'd said something funny only nobody laughed. They'd all just turned and looked at her.

Maybe Staci had the right idea, there *was* some kind of a disease. Everybody could just look at you and tell if you'd got it. If you were immature.

Phoebe thought about having a disease. It would be like in elementary school, when nobody would touch anything that belonged to Tamás Horvath. On the playground flocks of girls would swoop by him, screeching, spinning him around in the tail of their flight. "You've got

To-mash Hor-vath's cooties!" they sang, and everybody scattered before them.

"I never did that," Phoebe whispered.

But she did. She'd chased Staci Boyd, screaming just like the others.

Phoebe hung her head way down over the water. Her ears were ringing so she could barely hear the sound of the river. She tried to swallow, but it seemed her throat wouldn't work in that position. A drop of spit spun away into the water.

I'm having a stroke, she thought.

She meant to say the words out loud, as if speaking aloud would break the spell that clamped down on her. But if any words came out she did not hear them, only the shrilling and pounding in her ears. She couldn't feel her feet, either, if they were still touching the road.

Then she was afraid. The water shone darkly, like metal. The water and sky were shrinking in around her, cold and colorless and without air. The chill tightened the skin of her temples until her eyes stretched wide open.

Phoebe kicked out with her feet, thrashed with her arms. She barely felt her legs scrape over the rail. She was falling off the bridge.

The sky exploded in fragments, and the black cold sucked her down. Phoebe struggled like a newborn puppy, clogged and blinded by the cold. Then suddenly she no longer felt it. She felt fire—her veins were running with fire. She struck out, trying to swim, feeling her limbs light as flames, but without force.

The current spun her toward the rocks at the shallow end of the swimming hole. In a minute she ground against them, bumping an ankle, skinning her knuckles. She grabbed for handholds between shifting stones, crawled out on hands and knees over the weed-slicked rocks.

A thin breeze stiffened her clothes. The cold seemed to have soaked right down to her bones and made them ache. Phoebe shuddered all over, like a wet dog.

Wonderful!... Oh, God, she felt so wonderful—she could feel life barreling down every shadowy pathway of her inside self. And above her the sky stretched high and blue and ruffled with white clouds. Phoebe laughed out loud. The sound came out all funny, like troll music.

She squished up the bank to Steephill Road, knowing she had to get home quickly, get some dry things. Water trickled down the side of her nose from her hair. *Why did people always say water doesn't have any smell?* She put up her hand to wipe it away.

It was only then that she noticed her numbed fingers were clenched around a rock from the river.

Except that it wasn't a rock but a thick chunk of glass—like a fragment broken from the river itself. The first thing she did was hold it up to the light.

She could see through it, sort of. She could hardly tell just what she was seeing. The images came to her at odd angles and distorted, rimmed with prism colors. Phoebe started uphill, forgetting about the school bus, scarcely noticing even where she went, her head bent over the glass.

Near the top of the hill she turned and looked back at the bridge. Why had she been so afraid before? There was nothing there. Seen through the glass, the bridge railing seemed to snake up into the sky. She could hardly tell the river from the sky. It made her feel as if she were falling again, but falling slowly, falling upward, like a bubble.

Then she saw the man. A trick of the curving glass made him appear suddenly very close, though she hadn't noticed him at all before. He was dressed in black and had a long beard that flowed over his chest. The beard seemed to pick up the fiery colors from the prisms in the glass. And he was looking back at her. It was almost as if he were inside the glass, she saw him so clearly. His mouth opened to say something. She could tell he was furiously angry. He raised one fist that clutched a tall black staff.

Phoebe's hand fumbled with the glass, and she lost the image.

There really was a man, but it was only Mr. Barnes, and he was all the way down the hill on his own lawn. His face was smooth and pink. He wore powder blue slacks with a plaid jacket. In his hand was his groundskeeper's stick with the nail in the end. He used it now to stab up a leaf that had blown onto his lawn.

CHAPTER II

Phoebe Van der Clute

> A thousand thoughts she fashioned in her mind,
> And in her feigning fancie did pourtray
>
> —*The Faerie Queene*, III, 4

PHOEBE BENT OVER THE TREASURE cupped in her hand. Even in the dark of the stair landing, her pale reflection seemed to float above its polished surface. The reflection made her eyes appear shadowy and dramatic. Ordinarily they were just bland, baby-doll blue. *And my lashes are too light, so I look surprised all the time,* Phoebe thought. She liked the dark-eyed image in the glass.

She turned the piece of glass over. The other side was where it had been broken. Maybe when the glass was whole it had been all round and polished, like a crystal ball. She raised it to her eye and tried to look through the broken side. Of course, there was nothing to see now, with the light off on the stairs.

Downstairs the telephone made its little *ping*. Her mother had ended her conversation. Now she was moving around, running water in the kitchen, getting her coat out of the hall closet.

"Hurry up and *leave*," muttered Phoebe, willing her. "You have to *leave now*, or you'll be late for rehearsal."

Althea played principal viola with the Wintersham College Camerata. This spring they were rehearsing the Bartók viola concerto, which meant a rare solo opportunity for her. The Bartók solo was practically all Althea had time to think about anymore.

So probably she'd already forgotten sending Phoebe upstairs to fetch her Orchestra binder. Althea had said she wanted to see the music Mrs. Gorton passed out in Orchestra for the Junior Philharmonic tryouts. All during supper she'd dwelt alarmingly on that subject.

Supper was cream of celery soup and western omelette, which meant mainly scrambled eggs with ketchup. Althea Van der Clute was not interested in food. She was not interested in a lot of things, among them shopping, meals, and excuses. What interested her was perfection, and perfection was music.

"Is Mrs. Gorton going to make you sight-read?" she'd asked Phoebe. "Did you get her to show you the cross-fingerings for that high F sharp?"

Phoebe excused herself and began scraping her plate into the garbage.

"Phoebe, I can't hear a word you're saying over that clatter."

"Actually, I have a lot of Civics homework tonight," Phoebe said. "Maybe I better get started."

Althea pushed back her gray curls, which were beginning to frizz out of their careful waves. "Phoebe, life is too short for this nonsense. Go get your books. And bring me that music, too."

So Phoebe had thundered up the stairs, then sat down quietly on the top step to wait. There was no point in switching on the light to look for her backpack with her music binder. It was not upstairs. She'd left it—and, she suddenly realized, her clarinet case, too—on the gravel by the foot of the Steephill Road bridge. She'd forgotten all about her stuff when she fell into the river.

And now a terrible thought struck Phoebe. Who had her mother been talking to on the phone? What if her mother had phoned Mrs. Gorton? Oh, God, she'd only wanted just a little extra time—the weekend, to practice in—before facing Mrs. Gorton again. She'd forgotten all about those stupid tryouts. And now—oh, God, *God*—what if it rained again tonight, and her clarinet got ruined?

Why hadn't she had the sense to stay in the toolshed? She'd planned to spend the whole day safe in the toolshed, with a book and her lunch and the rain drumming on the roof.

But by midday the rain had blown away. Sequins of light filtered through the dark roof of the shed. Phoebe had started flipping through the pages of her book to see if there were any good parts left before the ending. She had already read the ending.

That was when she'd decided to go to the river. Behind the toolshed the ground dropped steeply down a wooded bank. All the houses on River Road were built at the top of the bank. There wasn't even a footpath through the trees to the water.

Phoebe set her feet sideways, using half-buried rocks or catching at brush to break her downhill slither. She knew the steep slope hid her from view of the house windows.

She wanted to check on her Civilization on the riverbank. There'd been so much rain the last few days, probably the People had suffered some awful disaster.

When she got to the bottom, she saw she was right. The cottages along the harborside were all waterlogged. The one with the watchtower was completely ruined, and Giles the Watchman missing.

"Swept away by the raging flood," she said aloud.

Then she thought maybe Giles was a too romantic name for a night watchman. Giles the Poet. Giles the Troubadour... Maybe Giles had been in love with somebody before he met his tragic destiny.

Phoebe knelt on a flat rock by the water's edge. The river was still high. Trout lilies bloomed under the surface like the gaudy-colored fish of coral seas. But the water was icy. It made her fingers ache if she left them in too long. Phoebe ran her wet fingers through her hair, forking thick warm red curls off the back of her neck.

At school some kids in her class had started calling her Brillohead, and now they were all doing it. It was no big deal, lots of kids got nicknames. Anyway, it was better than Van der Klutz.

Maybe Giles the Watchman had been in love with Angelina the Fisher Maid. Only, it was a hopeless love, because secretly Angelina was betrothed to the Prince. But Angelina was not yet ready to leave the freedom of the fisher's life, or the simple cottage that she tended for her father, Old Angelo the Fisherman. Phoebe could see a glint of gold where the Prince stood in a twist of the castle turret, overlooking the harbor. She set him down on the village green beside a group of soggy villagers.

Then she noticed the footprints, three of them, in the soft forest earth at the edge of the path that ran along the riverbank. A fourth print was no more than the half-moon of a heel. The rest of the foot had come down squarely on the moss thatch of Old Angelo's cottage.

Phoebe pawed through the crumbled moss and mud bricks, searching for the bright blue of Angelina's dress. Angelina was not there. Whoever stepped on the house must have picked her up. Some kid... No one else would have bothered.

Phoebe pictured herself falling down on the cold earth of the path, sobbing for Angelina. By squinting, she could almost bring up tears. *The trouble with me*, thought Phoebe, *is I ate my lunch too early*. Yawning, she bundled the villagers into their houses and set the Prince back in the tall, rot-riddled stump that was the Royal Castle.

"He is distraught," she said. "This is a terrible crisis."

In fact he did look rather cockeyed. The weather had softened his glue. That was Staci's fault; she always used too much glue, so it didn't set up right.

Phoebe and Staci Boyd had made the People together, out of the pink plastic pins Phoebe's mother used to skewer her hair curlers. The curler pins had knobs on the top, which made them look like people with round pink faces. The girls had cut the pins into different lengths and dressed them with scraps of cloth, cotton wool, glitter, and glue. In time the People had developed stories all their own that came from the hazards of being outdoors. Like the flood at the harbor. Knowing they were outside alone at night was what made the People not just toys.

Only, now Angelina was lost, and the Prince was coming unglued. And Staci Boyd didn't want to play anymore.

The front door banged, jolting Phoebe back to her immediate problems. Althea had gone. So she *couldn't* have phoned Mrs. Gorton—not and just left like that, without saying a word ... So Phoebe still had time—time to get her stuff from the bridge, time to persuade Pop to sign an absence excuse for school. She would write the note and get Pop to sign it. And then she'd have to go back to the bridge, to get her stuff. Tonight. *Now* . . .

Here Phoebe paused for a couple of deep breaths. That man at the bridge—was it possible she'd exaggerated, somehow, the way he'd looked? Not made it up, but just exaggerated? The black staff and the flaming beard—she'd only seen them through the piece of glass. That's what had made her think the glass was magic.

CHAPTER III

Archimago

With faire discourse the evening so they pass:
For that old man of pleasing wordes has store,
And well could file his tongue as smooth as glas.
—*The Faerie Queene*, I, 1

PHOEBE CAME DOWNSTAIRS SLOWLY and loitered at the door of the living room.

"Pop? Can you sign something for me, for school?"

He didn't answer. He was reading, with the lamp switched on over his chair, though there was still plenty of light at seven o'clock on a spring evening. The late sunlight spilled through the picture window and lay at his feet like a neglected dog.

Phoebe came and fluttered the absence excuse under his nose. Pop scribbled his signature, using his book for a desk.

"What's this?" he asked, handing the paper back to her.

"A permission slip," she told him, "for school. What are you reading?"

"Book One, One."

He meant the first chapter in Book One of Spenser's *Faerie Queene*. There were six complete books, and each one had twelve chapters that were called cantos. Phoebe knew the code. Her father was an authority on the Elizabethan poet Edmund Spenser and had been a professor of sixteenth-century literature at the college before he had his stroke. Now he was sort of retired.

"Remember when you used to read that to me, at bedtime?"

"Oh, yes."

"It's funny, I never thought about it being poetry. I just liked all the knights and quests, you know? The fairy-tale stuff."

Pop turned the page. Phoebe sighed and fiddled with her piece of glass. She didn't feel ready to go back to the bridge yet.

She said, "I used to pretend like I was that lady knight, you know? Britomart." In the story Britomart looked into Merlin's magic glass and fell in love with a knight she saw there. Then she went to Faeryland and had a lot of adventures looking for him. "And Staci always wanted to be Fair Amoret, or else Florimel, that all the knights were always fighting over..." Her voice trailed off.

She tried reading over Pop's shoulder:

> For that old man of pleasing wordes had store,
> And well could file his tongue as smooth as—

But the old man in the story turned out to be Archimago the Evil Enchanter in disguise. Archimago was always disguising himself to trap people. Or he'd conjure beautiful ladies out of thin air, to tempt them.

Pop rubbed his ear where she was breathing on it. "You could read it to yourself now," he said.

"I don't know... There's too many footnotes. It was better when you read it. You know all the good parts."

Pop hadn't any answer to that, but Phoebe didn't mind. She felt cozy, leaning against his chair, chatting about books and stuff.

"Anyway," said Phoebe, "it's no good since I found out it's all just supposed to be allegory. Like when Prince Arthur is fighting that giant, what's-his-name—"

"Orgoglio?"

"Yeah, and there's blood gushing all over the place, and it's mushed into the dirt and gore over the tops of his shoes. And then he cuts off Orgoglio's head and, like, all of a sudden the giant just vanishes—I used to think that was so amazing. But if the giant is just supposed to stand for pride, and Arthur is the Christian man overcoming pride . . . Like, pride couldn't *really* kill you, see what I mean? It was better when I thought it was a real story."

"Spenser would have said that the allegory is the real story. The life of the mind is real. The knight and the giant are just appearances."

"But it's not a *real giant* if it's just supposed to stand for something else. I mean, pride couldn't bleed all over your shoes, right?"

Pop steepled his fingers together and addressed the picture window, as if he were giving a college lecture to a bunch of strangers.

"Spenser thought of allegory as a kind of magic glass," he said. "The idea comes from Saint Paul in the Bible, who tells us that we see the truth 'as through a glass, darkly.' Spenser wanted his imagination to work for us like that dark glass. We're supposed to look through the poetic images to the true reality."

Phoebe wasn't satisfied. "I thought reality was supposed to be, like, the opposite of imagination." Reality was what you saw when you *weren't* imagining things.

"Pop," she said, "listen, Pop— What if you had a real magic glass? Do you think it would work the same way? Show you the truth, I mean."

But he didn't answer. His eyes had gone back to the page. Phoebe held up her piece of glass and looked around the room through it. She saw the square of light from the window, repeated three or four times. The squares revolved as she turned the glass, like lighted cars on a Ferris wheel.

"Listen," she said, joggling Pop's arm to get his attention. "How do you know if you're seeing it right? Because when you look through glass, sometimes things look all strange. How do you know you aren't tricked?"

"That's why they give you the footnotes, I suppose." Pop smiled, but not at Phoebe. At the pages of his book. He thought they were still talking about the book.

Phoebe looked at him through the broken glass. But she couldn't get it lined up right or something, because she couldn't see Pop at all.

She decided not to tell him that she was going out. He wasn't listening to her, anyway.

It's like an adventure, thought Phoebe, to make herself feel brave. To make it more like an adventure she took the river path back to the bridge instead of Steephill Road. As the light faded out of the sky, her feeling of adventure grew, faster than the bravery. Now she remembered the man at the bridge very clearly, and began to wonder if maybe she hadn't exaggerated how her mother might take the bad news about the clarinet.

Phoebe dawdled. There was a place beside the path where she liked to linger; she called it the Enchanted Glade. You had to know the right way to look to recognize the Glade. The strip of woodland along the water grew broader and less tangled the closer you got to the bridge. That was because the bank wasn't so steep. Then, just before the woods ended at the swimming hole, there was a ring of pale beech trees.

And inside the circle of the trees there were bluebells that bloomed white. Maybe the beech roots sucked the blue from the flowers; beeches are hungry trees. Or maybe the blue was still there, unseen but scented in the air inside the magic circle.

There was music, too, in the Enchanted Glade. Phoebe had heard it several times, a single flute that trickled through the gray limbs of the beeches like rain.

Though really, thought Phoebe, *the music must come from the Horvaths' house. Theirs is the closest.*

She was stepping extra carefully, as she always did in the Glade. There were some boggy places where the soft covering of fallen leaves would sink and her shoes fill up with mud.

The music was probably just ordinary, like from the TV, only it carried oddly through the woods. Like sometimes when a car goes by with the stereo turned up loud, but you only hear the boom of the bass, not the singing. Phoebe listened for the music.

She listened until she could hear the air rustling inside her ears, but that was all. The silence spooked her a little. It was odd how, in the Enchanted Glade, even the friendly noise of the river was stilled. Phoebe looked back the way she had come, through the trees. It was almost dark now, but she could see a silvery trail of bent-over stems from the whitebells.

This was the only place she knew to find the white-bells. And once, years ago, she had found a ring here.

It had been a brass ring, with a treble clef stamped in the place where the stone ought to go. Phoebe had willed so hard for it to be a magic wishing ring that odd things had begun to happen. Or almost begun—it was really more of a willing ring. Phoebe's mother had seen the greenish stain on her finger, and the raw place where the metal chafed. She told Phoebe to throw it away. She said it would give her blood poisoning.

The brass ring reminded Phoebe of the chunk of glass in her jacket pocket. *Somehow,* she thought, *somewhere in the world, real magic must be possible. It must!* Her fingers tightened over the glass. Why wasn't it?

Everything was so unfair. She'd waited all her life for magic that was never really going to happen, at least not to her. Maybe she was the wrong kind of person... She couldn't do all those things people did in adventures, like ride a horse or shinny up trees. She felt as if the real wishing ring and the real magic looking glass had gone away someplace together, leaving her behind.

Phoebe found her backpack and the clarinet right where she'd left them, on the gravel beside the bridge.

"Thank goodness for that," she said, slipping the backpack over her shoulders.

She took a quick look under the bridge in case there was anyone lurking around, but it was too dark now to see much. Anyway, there wasn't anybody.

She saw the lights were on at the Barn Marché across the bridge. Mr. Barnes often stayed open late on Friday and Saturday. *What if I went in there?* thought Phoebe. *What if I looked at him through the glass?* Because it was just too stupid to sneak out at night and not have anything happen at all.

Though Mr. Barnes made it clear that he didn't like kids coming into his store, not even around Mother's Day, when you might actually buy something. Not that he was rude, exactly—not like old Mrs. Park at the Pay 'n' Save, who only let kids come in one at a time in case you stole. Mr. Barnes just hovered around with his hands kind of quivering, waiting to catch whatever it was you finally dropped.

He could be in disguise, like Archimago, thought Phoebe, walking up the bank to the road. His store was just the kind of place Archimago might like. Villains always put their castles right at the end of a bridge, so they could fight you when you tried to cross over.

What really bothered her was going out on the bridge again. She stopped and rubbed the place on her stomach where, before, the bridge rail had pressed so hard.... It was like having a stitch in her side. A little stitch of fear. But it was nothing like the awful, creeping dread she'd felt that afternoon. She ran across, with one hand clenched over her stomach and the clarinet case banging her knee.

At the Barn Marché, even the bell that tinkled above the door was made of glass. Mr. Barnes glanced up from the package he was gift-wrapping for a lady in a yellow dress. He frowned, but what could he do, with his fingers stuck in the bow? All the same, Phoebe put her hands behind her back and moved quickly to get out of his line of sight.

The store was in the two main downstairs rooms of Mr. Barnes's house. The rooms were one behind the other, connected by a wide-open archway, so it was almost like one long room. There was a picture window in the front and a big plate-glass mirror on the back wall of the second room. The mirror reflected the window, and across the store the window glass reflected the mirror. The double reflections made the space in between seem curiously unreal.

Phoebe stepped carefully through a forest of spindly-legged tables, every one freighted with objects of glass. Rows of chandeliers hung twinkling from the ceiling. Her reflection followed her down the room, catching and sliding over polished surfaces.

She paused by a display of spun-glass animals. There used to be a man at the Danbury Fair who made those for people, right there while you watched. But these were much more elaborate and lacy. That dragon looked like it'd break a wing if you only just thought about it too hard. *Besides, I don't like its beady eyes*, thought Phoebe, moving on.

In a corner of the back room, pushed up against a window, she found a table of glass paperweights. A notice on a piece of folded card read, FOR DISPLAY ONLY. NOT FOR SALE.

They certainly were amazing paperweights. Each one had a tiny fairy-tale character trapped in a bubble inside the glass. Phoebe bent down to examine the most perfect little pink princess. Her hair was like a breath of gold mist under the veil of her tall pointed pink hat. And see, she had the teeniest silver slippers just peeping out from the swirl of her skirt. *That's the way Angelina would look, if she ever really did marry the Prince*, thought Phoebe.

Next her glance fell on a little fat wizard in a blue robe spangled with stars. Phoebe reached out her hand for him, then thought better of it and tiptoed over to where she could see Mr. Barnes in the mirror. He was looking the other way, still busy with the lady customer—good. Phoebe hurried back to the table of paperweights. She just had to pick one up.

The glass ball was no bigger than a largish orange, but

quite heavy. And it was all the way round; the plain metal ring that had kept it from rolling off the table turned out to be a separate piece, a stand. The glass had a green tinge that gave the character inside an underwater look.

The little wizard reminded Phoebe of Pop, in a funny way. Pop would make a good Merlin, with plaid house slippers on under his starry robe. Very gently she set the Merlin ball back into its ring.

Now here was an interesting thing. The ball closest to the window had left a streak of mist on the window glass behind it. You might almost believe it had been breathing on the windowpane. The figure in the ball was a knight in shining armor on a white charger. *Poor thing, he must be weary of his glass prison*. He was longing to look out. On an impulse Phoebe picked up the ball with its metal base and carried it over to the display of fairground animals. Maybe they'd cheer him up a little. Then she went back to the other paperweights.

The next one to catch her eye had some kind of an animal inside. Phoebe picked it up to get a closer look. It was not just an animal but a faun, the Greek myth kind: half goat and half boy. The boy was naked to the waist and playing on a flute. His crooked goat's legs kicked up in a dance.

She held the ball to her ear but felt only the cool touch of glass; no music, of course. Though he looked so merry and so real, it was hard to believe that if she broke the glass the music wouldn't come tumbling out. She shook the ball, as if that would make the music swirl around, like the snowstorm in a Christmas globe. The glass slipped in her fingers, and she almost dropped it.

Oh, God, just what she needed was to smash some valuable antique, when she wasn't even supposed to be out of the house. Phoebe set the paperweight back in its place and jammed her hands into her pockets.

There in her pocket was her own piece of glass. And look—it was the same greenish color as the paperweights, with a couple of tiny bubbles trapped in the glass, like soda fizz. Like the paperweights. Phoebe turned her broken piece over and over in her fingers. One side round and polished. The other broken ... But see here—here was a little smooth dimple in the broken side, where there might once have been a bigger bubble. Or a place to put a miniature figurine.

Phoebe set her piece next to the ball with the pink princess. The glass looked just the same. The princess's hand was raised in an airy gesture, as if to say, *I told you so*. Phoebe brought the broken piece to her eye and looked through.

At first she had trouble spotting the paperweights. There were so many bright things in the room, that all seemed to be jumping around in the glass. Phoebe bent right over the table, searching for the scrap of pink that was the princess. There! She'd got her lined up right now. She could even see the tiny character inside, with her hand lifted—

No, the hand was actually pressing on the glass wall of the paperweight!

Phoebe thumped down on her knees to be at eye level with the princess ball. The princess's hand was definitely right against the glass. Phoebe could see the pale tips of her fingers where they pressed. She couldn't see the face so clearly, because—because the princess was breathing on the glass. A minute patch of fog hid her face.

"Wipe it off," whispered Phoebe. And sure enough, the pink girl raised her other hand, and—

"What do you think you are doing!"

Mr. Barnes! She'd forgotten all about him. Phoebe scrambled to her feet so fast she almost upset the table.

"Don't you know better than to touch these things?" He rushed toward her with hands raised like plump sails. Then he stopped, stock-still, and slowly pointed an accusing finger. "What is that in your hand?"

His voice slid up the register while his glasses slid down to the tip of his nose. But he was not funny. Phoebe could see white all the way around the pale blue centers of his eyes.

"Did you break something?"

Phoebe gabbled, "Oh no, I didn't break anything, really, I hardly touched—I mean, look—it's just a bit of old bottle glass, it's not from here—"

This was awful. This was awfuller than Phoebe could possibly have imagined. Mr. Barnes was still fixing her with that pointing finger. She held the piece of glass up, as if it would protect her.

"Give . . . that . . . to . . . me." His pink lips lifted and fell with the words, but his teeth stayed locked in a mean line.

Phoebe stared at Mr. Barnes. Was he crazy or something? She hadn't done anything bad. She didn't want to give him her glass. His little angry reflection slid over the polished surface in her hand. She held the piece of glass up to her eye and looked through.

A sudden brilliance made her blink. The stiffly pointing figure before her seemed to suck up all the light in the room, leaving the rest dark. His eyes flared. His fiery beard tumbled over his breast. His teeth were locked in a grimace of indescribable fury.

Phoebe turned to run, ducking to avoid the hand that she knew, without daring to look, was now stretched out to seize her. She heard a bump and a shriek. Her backpack had hit the table with the paperweights.

She whirled and made a grab for the table, but in her confusion only succeeded in knocking it again with her clarinet case. The glass balls rolled everywhere. Mr. Barnes, now perfectly ordinary-looking again, launched himself at the little table in an attempt to catch it before it toppled.

But he was too late, or perhaps he banged it again in his rush. A ball rolled right over his clutching hand and smacked into the window glass.

Then everything turned to pandemonium. Mr. Barnes was screaming like a woman—unless that was the lady in the yellow dress. She'd come into the room with the gift-wrapped package in her hands and was now actually standing on another table, shrieking at the top of her lungs.

Because there was an animal in the store. Something big and brown was bounding around the room, crashing into glass. Was it a dog that had got in, or—

Mr. Barnes tried to throw his sportscoat over its head as it charged past him. The animal veered and collided with a table of colored bottles. Phoebe backed into a chandelier that clanked around her ears.

Mr. Barnes was yelling and flapping his arms. The animal leapt clear over a fallen whatnot and raced down the room toward the little window in the back.

Phoebe fled for the door. Seconds later her feet were pounding over the bridge. Behind her, faintly, came the sounds of shouts and smashing window glass.

CHAPTER IV

The Faun

They mocke and scorne him, and him foule miscall;
Some by the nose him pluckt, some by the taile,
And by his goatish beard some did him haile:
Yet he (poore soule) with patience all did beare;
For, nought against their wils might countervaile:
Ne ought he said what ever he did heare;
But hanging downe his head, did like a Mome appeare.

—*The Faerie Queene*, VII (unfinished), 6

IT WAS SATURDAY MORNING. Althea sat alone at the breakfast table. She leaned on her hand and stirred her coffee but didn't drink it. When Phoebe brought over her own cereal bowl, Althea took her elbow off the table.

"Good morning," she said.

"Morning. D'you know where my jean jacket is? I stuck it in the dryer yesterday, but now I can't find it."

"I hung it out on the line. The dryer isn't working properly."

"Not again!"

"I'm surprised you didn't notice; it was making a terrible grating noise. That was the first thing I heard when I got in last night."

"I didn't hear a thing."

"Neither did your father, apparently. You two! What does it take to make you and Francis notice anything?"

Phoebe didn't answer because she had to concentrate on pouring the milk to the brim of her bowl without spilling. Her cereal never looked like the picture on the box, all studded with glistening raspberries. When she was little she'd believed the raspberries were supposed to be in the box, too.

"Where is Pop?" she asked.

"He had a bad night. I hope he'll stay in bed this morning."

Phoebe nodded, her throat clogged with bran flakes.

Her mother said, "Phoebe, about your music—" There were sharp little pleats at the corners of Althea's mouth, as if her words had a bitter taste. "I think it's time you and I and Sally Gorton got together and had a talk."

Phoebe forced down her mouthful of cereal. It was like swallowing a wad of Kleenex. "Okay—but first I really need to, uh—I mean, you need to help me on one piece. That Charles Ives—I never seem to get my breaths right on that piece." She sneaked a sideways glance at her mother. "Maybe we better wait till after Pop gets up, okay?"

Althea's eyes had a queer, too-bright look, like glass beads. She was stirring her coffee some more.

"You're going to make that cold," Phoebe told her.

Althea picked up her cup and took a sip, then set it down again. Probably it was stony cold. "After he gets up..." she repeated dully. "We shouldn't disturb him now."

Althea didn't look like she'd had too good a night herself, thought Phoebe, as she rinsed out her bowl. What was the *matter* with everybody these days? Pop was a zombie. Althea jittered all over the place—except, now she was just sitting, staring at her coffee spoon like she was totally unplugged.

On an impulse Phoebe pulled out her piece of glass and looked through it at her mother. But Althea appeared the same as always. She'd forgotten to set her hair. Her fuzzy curls were escaping the nylon scarf.

Phoebe put the glass back in her pocket and went out to the clothesline, feeling oddly comforted.

The clothesline ran on pulleys from the top of the back porch out across the lawn. Phoebe hauled out a laundry basket and the cut-off bleach jug for clothespins and began taking down laundry.

Luckily it hadn't rained again. Even so, some of this stuff still felt damp. Phoebe tossed a couple of pins into the jug. She liked the squeak of the pulleys as the rope ran through them. The clothespins looked like people going up and down a ski lift. Or a ramp... hauling stuff up and down a ramp. They were slaves, working on... on building a pyramid. Every day they were forced to haul backbreaking loads up and down this dangerous narrow ramp—

"*Psst!*"

Phoebe looked around to see where the noise had come from, but there wasn't anything.

So, anyway, the Evil Overseer didn't know that secretly the clothespin slaves were planning an escape. One by one on this fatal morning, as they reached the bottom of the ramp, they were slipping away... to a little boat... Phoebe dropped more clothespins into the jug.

"*Psst!*"

Phoebe frowned. She worked faster, bundling the clothes without folding them into the basket. The Evil Overseer was getting suspicious, because—

"*Psst! Pssst!*"

She yanked her jacket off the line. The last two pins popped off and were lost in the grass.

"Who's there!"

"Here—in the bush." A yew bush at the end of the lawn rustled.

"Well, come *out* of there. Who are—Tamás!"

Tamás Horvath's head poked out of the yew bush. For

some reason he had a bright green scarf wrapped around his head, like a gypsy fortune-teller.

"You were spying on me!" Phoebe said angrily. "How long were you hiding in there?"

Tamás gaped at her. It was like when she was in third grade and the Horvaths first came to live on River Road. Tamás used to stand at the end of her driveway and just stare—stare at the house, at her, at the driveway, at nothing. Sometimes he carried his baby sister in his arms. He'd had eyes like empty windows and always a line of snog crawling down his lip.

They'd put Tamás in her class at school, though he was bigger and probably older than the other kids. In those days he came to school every day in a brown leather cap like a helmet, with a tiny visor and flaps that hung down over his ears. If the chin strap was snapped, Tamás's mouth stayed closed. If it was unsnapped his chin dangled. Before he did the straps he always pushed his chin up with his fingers. Then he said, "Boop-boop!" Like that was supposed to mean a job well done.

Boop-boop! Phoebe smiled to herself. She'd almost forgotten about that.

"All night," said Tamás, breaking into her recollections.

"What?"

"All night I was hiding in this bush." He gave her his long, V-shaped smile, but it looked dried on, like leftover breakfast egg. His eyes were pink rimmed, with dark shadows under them.

"Tamás, what are you talking about? You couldn't be in there all night. It was practically freezing."

"Yes."

"Look, Tamás—I'm not trying to be mean or anything, but why don't you just go home, okay? I'm busy today."

"No." He shook his head and went on shaking it. "No, no."

It was odd, Tamás was still in some of her classes, but she felt like she hadn't really looked at him for years. He'd changed a lot from the round-faced little boy in the leather helmet. There were hollows under his cheekbones, and his long, narrow nose had a bend in it. It must have got broken sometime. Only his eyes were the same, dark and blank and curiously tilted at the corners.

"I'm sorry," said Phoebe, trying to be nice, "did your mother send you over here for something?"

Mrs. Horvath was always running out of things. She didn't drive, and she hardly spoke any English. Once every other week a lady from Social Services drove her over to Wintersham to do some marketing, but between trips she ran out of things. At first she'd come herself to knock at the Van der Clutes' door, humbly holding out her little cup for sugar or rice. Nowdays they rarely saw her; she sent Tamás, or more often cute little Eva, to do her borrowing.

"Come into the kitchen and I'll get you what you need," said Phoebe.

"No, I can't do that."

He raised his hands to the scarf on his head and she saw that he was wearing a violently patterned Hawaiian shirt several sizes too wide. She recognized the shirt; it was the one the English department staff had given Pop for a joke at his retirement party. Althea must have hung it out on the line. And that green scarf—

"That's Althea's scarf!"

Tamás blushed, a slow, painful blush that reddened even his eyelids, as if he had been crying. He stood up then, but still he wouldn't come out of the yew bush. He clutched at the dark branches like somebody caught by surprise in the shower.

"Well, come on." Phoebe tried to keep her voice nice. It was like coaxing an animal.

"No, don't come close!" Tamás blurted. "I can't—I don't have any pants."

"You *what*?"

"I mean, I don't have any legs. They aren't the right legs. You won't like this," he concluded miserably.

Then he did come out of the bush. He held on to the bottom of the Hawaiian shirt and tried to pull it down as far as possible. But there was no hiding those legs. They were the woolly, crooked, cloven-hooved hind legs of a goat.

Phoebe's own legs and the bottom of her stomach felt like they'd been flushed. "Oh ... Tamás ..." She folded slowly onto the grass. "Give me a minute, okay? I'll be okay in a minute."

But it was more like five minutes before she took a long, shuddery breath and said, "How—how did it happen?"

He looked at her out of the corner of his eye. "You know."

Phoebe shook her head. How could she know? She could scarcely even breathe. She reached out her hand to him but couldn't, *couldn't* touch him.

"The scarf," she whispered, "do you ... ?"

Tamás dragged the bright scarf off his head. He had thick curly brown hair that failed to hide the nubs of young horns sprouting from his forehead. He had goaty ears, too.

Then, holding his hands poised to play on an invisible flute, Tamás began to dance. The crooked goat legs capered, the Hawaiian shirt flapped. He had a little tight-curled tail that whirled like a cheerful flag.

Phoebe cried, "Oh, God, you're the faun in the paperweight!"

Tamás stopped prancing and bowed to her, his slant-eyed face tilted up in a fey grin. The shadows under his eyes showed dark as bruises.

"But, Tamás, what *happened*?"

"You broke the glass. Last night, don't you remember? So then I jumped out the window and hid here. Until you came out."

This was all going by her too fast. She must be asking the wrong questions or something. She broke what glass? The paperweight? The window? No, Tamás must have broken Mr. Barnes's window himself, and then he came here and hid in the bush. "But why here?" she asked. "Why didn't you go home?"

"No. You don't understand."

"There's a *lot* I don't understand," said Phoebe. And she intended to find out. But not in the backyard, where Althea might decide to come out any minute, or even Mrs. Horvath might come by. She must be worried sick if Tamás had been gone all night.

"Let's go down to the river," she said. "We can talk there, and nobody'll bother us. And here—you'd better take this." She handed him the jean jacket. "It's a little damp still, but it'll dry pretty quick if you sit in the sun. I've got another jacket inside—just wait a minute while I fetch it, okay?"

He let her get almost through the door before he called her back. "Phoebe—"

"What is it?"

"Nothing. No, wait—do you think you can maybe get—something?"

"What kind of something?"

"Something . . . to eat."

"Oh, Tamás—I bet you're starving! I didn't think."

"Yes."

"I'll make some sandwiches, okay? For both of us. Is bologna all right?"

"All right . . ." He put his hands on his middle. "Do you think goats eat bologna? I don't know which half my stomach belongs to, you see."

"Wait here," said Phoebe.

It was turning out to be another beautiful spring day. Phoebe sat cross-legged on a rock beside the river while Tamás, squatting on his haunches like a dog, devoured all the sandwiches, Phoebe's as well as his own. They were peanut-butter-and-strawberry-jam, and cheese-with-pickle. When he had finished he licked the crumbs off the waxed paper and finally, experimentally, nibbled a corner of the paper.

"No good." He sighed. "I think my stomach is not goat." He folded the paper carefully and put it away under the jean jacket, in one of the pockets of Pop's Hawaiian shirt.

Phoebe couldn't help remembering one time—it was in third grade—when she was paper monitor. She was supposed to go along the aisles and pick up dictation papers. Tamás always sat by himself at the back of the classroom, because he couldn't be cured of muttering.

When she'd got to his seat she'd seen he was going over the lines of his paper with pencil, over and over, until the lines were slicks of graphite, his fingers grayed to the second knuckle. He hadn't written any dictation words. But he'd punctuated every line with a little crumpled pill of paper torn from the margin and pasted down with spit. Tamás had smiled as he handed her the damp paper. Phoebe had let him put it on the stack, then she'd dropped another on top so she wouldn't have to touch it.

He was smiling at her now. He almost always did smile, no matter what happened or what anybody said. And sometimes he used to kind of hum or buzz to himself, and his face made all these different expressions like he was having a conversation, only all inside himself. It was funny how she'd always just assumed he was happy, being like that. How could anyone be Tamás Horvath and be happy?

"Do you hate me?" said Tamás.

Phoebe felt her face getting hot. It was like he'd read her mind. "No, I don't hate you," she snapped. "Why would I do that?"

He shrugged. His long, big-knuckled fingers had begun plucking up clumps of moss.

"So why did you ask me that?"

Tamás rolled a little ball of moss between his fingers and sniffed it. He wouldn't meet her eyes. He said, "Well, I—I'm here, you know. And I don't—" He squashed the moss ball with his thumb. "I don't have any pants. And that's the sort of thing that happens to me, you know. You might hate that. I mean, I do."

"Look, Tamás—maybe we better concentrate on what we came down here for, okay? I want you to tell me the whole story. Do you think you can do that?"

Tamás flashed her an odd half smile, one eyebrow lifted, one corner of his mouth twisted up. He looked, just for a second, like some supersophisticated villain from an old black-and-white movie. Then he glanced away.

"What's the point?" he said. "You won't understand."

"Yes, I will, too. Because, look—" Phoebe pulled out her piece of glass and held it out to him. "Go ahead, look at it."

"Where did you get that?" He wouldn't take it from her hand.

Phoebe told him how she fell off the bridge, and found the piece of glass, and looked through it at Mr. Barnes. "He's the one that's doing it all, isn't he? He really is some kind of an enchanter."

Tamás nodded. "Every day when I was inside the ball, he used to come and look... I'd see his face, huge, looking in. Like a giant newborn pink rat. There were others, too, in the glass balls, but I don't know who. They were all changed, like me. Like people in a play."

"But how does he do it? And why?"

"I don't know. I thought about it a lot. I had a lot of time to think."

Phoebe said, "That's something else I don't understand. You said, like, every day he looked in. But how long were you in there?"

"Months, I think."

"But, Tamás, you couldn't be. I've seen you—talked to you, even. Or at least ... you've been in school."

"But did you talk to me, Phoebe? Did you? Did I act all the way okay?"

Phoebe looked at him helplessly. What could she say? He *never* acted all the way okay.

Tamás was picking at the wool on his goat legs now, twisting it around his fingers. "When I was inside the glass," he said, not looking at Phoebe, "I used to dream about my life—going to school, going home ... But maybe I was home, dreaming about ... dreaming ... Now I don't know which is the right Tamás. That's why ..."

"Why *what?*" Phoebe had to prompt him.

"Why I'm afraid to go home now."

Phoebe stared at him. It made her sick to think— She might've been going to school every day with some zombie calling itself Tamás Horvath. And those other people in the glass balls, who were they? There might be a bunch of zombies all over town....

Tamás was bending over Phoebe's piece of glass, which she'd set down on the moss between them.

"You, too," he said. "I think he tried to trap you, too."

Phoebe wasn't listening. There was a knight, she remembered, and a beautiful pink princess. Her first thought was that somehow the princess really was her kidnapped Angelina. But that wasn't possible, because however many weird things might be true, Phoebe had positively made up Angelina. So the princess had to be somebody else.

"What I think," said Tamás, "I think you falling off the bridge is what saved you. It broke the glass."

"Wait a minute. I'm thinking." Phoebe flapped her hand at him to tell him to be quiet.

Tamás was the faun. It was funny: now she thought about it, the image was exactly right for him—kind of silly, but kind of wild at the same time. Definitely not tame. It was like he'd been a faun all along, and she just hadn't noticed. So, who did she know who was like a princess? Or a knight— But she hadn't really looked carefully at him. She'd looked at the little wizard, Merlin.

Merlin, who'd reminded her of Pop.

"Phoebe, are you all right? Don't worry, Phoebe, you're all right now—"

Phoebe rubbed her hands over her eyes, as if that would rub away her terrible thought.

Tamás was up, clattering nervously around her on his little goat feet. "You're safe, Phoebe, please don't worry."

"Tamás, stop jumping around like that and tell me—tell me what you said about the glass again. I wasn't listening."

Tamás told her, standing stiffly before her with his

hands clutching the hem of the Hawaiian shirt, as if he were in front of the blackboard, giving a book report.

"So what I think is, the glass was clamping down on you but you fell in the water and it broke. Like if you heat up a marble in a fry pan and then drop it in a glass of water. Did you ever do that?"

"Tamás, that's really smart, you know that?"

Tamás shrugged. He had a trick of turning his face away and then looking back at her out of the tail of his eye. He really was like a wild animal sometimes.

Phoebe picked up the chunk of glass and held it out flat on her palm. Reflections swam over the surface. Right from the first she'd known it was magic.

"So what'll we do?" she said.

"Do—?"

"We have to do *something*. Think about all those other people trapped in the paperweights—and nobody even knows about them but us. We have to find out what's going on. We have to *rescue* them."

But Tamás had gone back to picking moss. He seemed to have lost interest in the whole subject.

"The secret must be in the glass," Phoebe said, mainly to herself. "We know it's magic, so we just have to find out how to use it. Isn't that the way it always works?" In books, that was the way magic worked. "Maybe if we could find the other pieces in the water. If we had the whole ball, we could wield the Power."

She gazed at the glass, as if expecting to see her fortune revealed there, as in a crystal ball. Like Britomart, the lady knight in *The Faerie Queene*, who gazed in Merlin's glassy globe and fell in love with the knight she saw there. Phoebe saw her own reflection.

And something more. Someone else. Another figure, seemingly behind her, was taking shape in the glass. But it was not Tamás. It was a knight on horseback.

CHAPTER V

SIR PARAVENT

Eftsoons there was presented to her eye
A comely knight, all arm'd in complet wize
—*The Faerie Queene*, III, 2

PHOEBE RUBBED HER HAND over the glass, but when she took it away the knight was still there, tiny and bright against a crisscross of dark branches. She bent forward, trying to get a better look. Her own reflected face filled up the glass. She rocked back on her heels, disappointed.

The image of the knight bloomed again on the surface of the glass. He appeared to be riding down a forest track—in some faraway country, maybe, like the knight that Britomart saw before she went to Faeryland and had all her adventures. There was—was that a second horse behind him? If only she could see!

Tamás kept skittering around, sharp ears pricked forward like a cat's.

"Tamás, for heaven's sake, stop—"

He snapped his fingers in her face and pointed. She frowned him away. Really, why did he have to act like such a goof?

"Yoy, Phoebe, behind you, look—look behind you!"

She flicked back a glance. "Oh my . . . God . . ."

There really was a knight. He was not in the glass but on the path behind her. She'd been fooled by the reflection. Phoebe put her hand over her mouth so it wouldn't hang open like Tamás's.

The knight's armor shone like moonlight on the shady path. Ostrich plumes crowned his helm, then curled, creamy as sea foam, down his steel-clad back. Even the horse wore armor, and a great sweep of cloth-of-silver caparisons that hid the movement of its legs.

The knight raised a mailed hand and pushed up his visor, revealing kingfisher blue eyes in a tanned face. He looked young. His cheeks were round and smooth, his lips smiling.

Phoebe put up her own hand in a small gesture that was not quite a wave. Actually, if Tamás had been standing a little closer she might have grabbed his arm.

She saw that the knight was leading a second horse, armored like his own but swathed in cloth the sunny color of polished copper. Phoebe felt a jolt of fear, thinking there was a body tied onto the saddle. But then she realized it was only an extra suit of armor. The legs and arms were strapped together in a bundle.

Both horses, the silver and the copper, came toward her with barely a jingle of harness, hardly the sound of a footfall. It was spooky, how quietly they moved.

It was the knight who, speaking courteously, broke the spell of silence. "Well met, Belphoebe, prowest maid alive," he hailed her.

"Why does he call you that?" muttered Tamás, close beside her now.

"Because—well, because that's my name, Belphoebe. It's something my father got out of a poem." Belphoebe was in *The Faerie Queene,* too, a maiden huntress, beautiful and fierce. But the name was terribly embarrassing. Phoebe never used it at school.

"So do you know this guy?"

"*Shh!* He'll hear you."

Now the knight was almost upon them. He checked his horse and dismounted all in one fluid movement, swinging his mail-clad leg over the horse's broad back and vaulting from the saddle. The wide bright plates of his armor made a sound like cymbals sliding together. Then in three long, spur-jingling strides he was before her and, incredibly, down on his knee.

"Who *is* this guy?" insisted Tamás.

The knight looked around in surprise, as if he'd only just noticed Tamás. He sprang athletically to his feet and bowed.

"Sir Paravent I hight," he said, taking Phoebe's hand. His own hands were covered over the tops with steel gauntlets, but underneath those their touch was warm and strong. "Archimago the Enchanter held me a prisoner of the glass until you, lovely championess, brake the glass and set me free." Then he kissed her hand.

Tamás said, "Huh!" But whether it was a question or he was just breathing through his mouth Phoebe couldn't tell.

Her hand felt like a bunch of red-hot sausages in the knight's firm clasp. She stammered, "Uh—please, will you let, uh— Oh! You must be the knight. *The knight in the paperweight*," she cried, turning to Tamás. "He must've got loose, too, last night after Mr. Barnes—" She swung back to Sir Paravent. "I'm so glad you did! And your poor horse, too."

In her excitement she almost put her other hand over his. Her fingers hovered an instant above the armored gauntlet.

Tamás put his head down so his silly little horns pointed rudely at the newcomer.

"He didn't say anything about Mr. Barnes," Tamás mumbled to the buttons of Pop's Hawaiian shirt. "He said somebody else . . . the Enchanter."

"Yes, that's what we thought." said Phoebe eagerly, to Sir Paravent. "I mean, we figured out who the Enchanter was—" Then she stopped, because she didn't understand why Paravent had said *Archimago*. Archimago was the enchanter who kept disguising himself in *The Faerie*

Queene. Did Lewis Barnes call himself Archimago? Or was he really Archimago, and only pretending to be Lewis Barnes? Phoebe opened her mouth to let out all the questions, then realized that Paravent was still squeezing her hand.

"Why—" she began, "I mean, who—"

Sir Paravent was gazing down on her face, his eyes half-closed in a lazy-looking smile. Yet somehow Phoebe was sure he was very wide awake.

He murmured, "Meseems I am taken prisoner once more—not of the glass, but of your crystal eyes."

Phoebe blushed. It was a blush so huge and hot it almost blew out her eardrums. Even Sir Paravent looked pink to her.

"Why don't you show him the piece of glass?" said Tamás, butting in.

Then Phoebe had to winkle her hand free, to get the glass from the ground where she'd left it.

"Uh, excuse me—I think you're standing on something of mine."

Paravent stepped back with a hasty exclamation of concern. He stooped to pick up the piece of glass, but Phoebe retrieved it first. She polished it, staring down at her reflected image until her face no longer felt on fire. In the reflection she appeared pale and serene, her eyes dramatically dark.

"See," she said, holding it up to Paravent, "we've got

this piece of the Enchanter's magic glass. "Tamás, he's the faun, he had this idea—"

Phoebe looked around to see if Tamás was going to help her with the explanations, but he had turned his back on the conversation. He was wandering around in his usual moonstruck manner, peering into the woods and patting at his pockets like Pop did when he'd lost his glasses.

Phoebe stumbled through the story the best she could by herself. All the time she was speaking she was conscious of Paravent's bright gaze. He stood so close to her he seemed to suck up all the oxygen in the air she was trying to breathe.

"... So you see," she said, getting to the end at last, "I found out about the Enchanter from the glass. Because if you look through it like this—"

"Stop!" cried Paravent, in a terrible voice. His face was pale as pudding beneath his gorgeous tan. "Lady, by the love I bear you, I beseech, never look brokenwise through the enchanted glass!"

"But I—"

He stopped her by touching his finger to her lips. "Know, fair Belphoebe, the glass is the Enchanter's eye, and where you look, he sees. And where he sees, he has the power to draw your image to himself, to imprison it in glass."

Phoebe's fingers curled around her bit of glass. She felt

like a snail shrinking into its shell. "Is that what he does," she said in a little voice, "steals people's ... images?"

"The image is the true self," answered Paravent. "It is the perfect model of the mind."

Phoebe said slowly, "I think I understand."

And she did think so. She'd noticed already about Tamás the faun—if you wanted to explain to somebody what Tamás was really like, you could hardly do better than to show the image of the half-wild creature he'd become through the glass. That must be what Pop had meant when they were having that talk about allegory—about how imagination shows you reality. He'd even called it a kind of dark glass. She wondered now what image the glass would have made of her own character.

Phoebe looked sadly at the broken piece in her hand. It was the only really and truly magic thing she'd ever owned. She said, "If I can't look through it, how can it help me?"

"It can only harm you, Belphoebe. Cast it away! Throw it into the river!" Paravent held out his hands to her in a gesture of appeal. "Let me help you."

"Oh no!" Phoebe stuck her hand with the glass behind her back. She heard a little hiss as Sir Paravent caught in his breath.

She couldn't look at him. Her eyes dropped to his shining breastplate, to the gilt buckles of his silver shoes. How could she act so rude, snatching the glass away as if she suspected him of trying to steal it?

"Try to understand," she begged. "It's not like I'm a knight or—or anything. The glass is all I've got. The only thing with any *power*. And I *need* the power, because I have to do something. I mean, about the other prisoners. I have to rescue them or something."

Phoebe knew she was explaining badly. But where could she find the words to tell about the little wizard with the starry robe? The one she'd called Merlin, but he reminded her of Pop—and when she'd tried to look at Pop through the enchanted glass, he wasn't there at all.

"It's like a quest I have to do," she said, raising her eyes to Paravent's.

A flush of pink had crept into his cheeks. "A quest!" His eyes fairly bulged with wonder. "Can these be women's words? What huge heroic magnanimity beats here, in the straight confine of a maiden's breast!"

"You, uh, you think you might want to join me?" Phoebe really wanted his help, but she wished he didn't have to mention her... body.

A sharp snort from Tamás, unexpectedly close to her ear, startled her.

"How come he talks like that?" said Tamás.

"I don't know! Because he's a knight, I guess."

"And another thing, where'd he get that extra horse? He didn't get that out of any paperweight."

"I don't *know*. Why don't you ask him?"

Sir Paravent had walked apart for a moment, perhaps out of delicacy, ignoring Tamás's rudeness. Or perhaps he'd needed time to consider Phoebe's proposition. Now he came forward again, leading the copper-colored horse, the one with the extra suit of armor.

"The horse is yours, Belphoebe, as it should have been," he said, "had you taken your place among the Enchanter's images as Britomart the Lady Knight." He began undoing the straps that held the bundled armor. "But now, make haste and arm yourself. The quest begins."

"Arm ...?" It took a moment for the horror of his suggestion to sink in. "What, you mean *in armor*? I can't do that! I mean, I don't even know how to ride!"

She watched, throat dry and palms moist, as he laid the steel-gray sections one by one on the grass, until they formed the shape of a man. Or of Britomart the Lady Knight.

"It was only a game," she protested. "I used to *play* I was Britomart."

Paravent named each piece of armor for her as he set it in place. "Sabotons," he said, setting out the pair of shoe covers. They had a long line of overlapping steel plates with spurs at the heels and sharp points for toecaps. They looked like a pair of metal scorpions lurking in the grass.

"Greaves ... poleyns ... cuisses ..." he recited, working up the body, "a fauld, to protect the hips; your tassets strap onto the fauld here ..."

Phoebe rubbed her palms down the sides of her jeans.

The helmet had a crest of white feathers like spilt milk. The hinged visor came to a sharp point and was punctuated with round holes.

"It looks like you should have rat whiskers," said Tamás, pushing up the visor to peer inside.

The visor clanked shut. The big sun-colored horse threw back its head at the noise and rolled its eye wickedly. Phoebe took a hasty step backward. But Tamás caught the horse by the bridle and spoke to it soothingly. The horse whuffled into his hair.

"Go on, talk to him, Phoebe," he urged. "Pet his neck. See how he loves it. There..."

Phoebe put up a timid hand. The horse felt very warm and solid. The golden hair ran smoothly all one way; you couldn't ruffle it like a cat's fur. *A palomino*, thought Phoebe. The sort of horse Britomart ought to ride.

"I only *wished* I was Britomart," she murmured.

She remembered one time when Jennifer Gorton had a pony party for her birthday. They'd all been really little then, of course. Phoebe had spilled something on her dress and cried, so Mrs. Gorton had to call Althea to come and take her home. But really Phoebe had only been afraid of the pony. Afterwards she was always a little shy of Mrs. Gorton, too.

Phoebe wished now she'd ridden the pony. The horse flicked its ears and shifted its feet, as if it sensed her nervousness.

"Do you know about horses, Tamás?"

"All Magyars know horses, it's in our blood. The Magyars," said Tamás, putting up his chin and looking down his long nose at her, "are men of Hungary. Not goats."

"Well, the reason I ask," said Phoebe, "the reason is, maybe you should be the one that's doing this. Because I'm not sure I can really—I mean, I never tried riding before. And this horse seems kind of antsy around me."

Sir Paravent pursed his lips. "It is a thing uncouth, and contrary to the honor of knighthood," he said, "that a beast should wield arms." He laid a broad shield in a brown canvas cover and a wicked-looking spear in the grass beside the empty armor.

Tamás said, "It's not you that worries the horse. There's something around here, in the woods. Or somebody. Don't you smell it?"

"I don't smell anything."

Phoebe caught a look from Paravent, who curled his lip and jerked his head at Tamás, like maybe he was what smelled.

"There's nobody here but us," she said.

Tamás put down his head stubbornly. "There are others," he insisted. "The horse knows. We animals understand about these things."

"It is wise to keep up your defenses," said Paravent. "Don the armor, Belphoebe."

"But can't Tamás do it? He can ride."

"Not with goat legs," said Tamás.

To begin with, Paravent made her put on a thick padded jacket slashed full of holes. The arming doublet, he called it. There were handfuls of brass-tipped laces to thread through the holes. The laces were used to tie on sections of armor.

"Begin at the bottom," Paravent advised, "and work up."

But after that he wasn't much help. He vaulted with incredible grace back into his high saddle. A wayward breeze flirted the creamy plumes of his helmet. He put up a steel-clad hand to brush them back. Then, half drawing the long blade that hung at his side, he occupied himself with patrolling the forest edge. "Let the beast act as squire," he called over his shoulder.

Phoebe slipped her arms through the leather straps of the breastpiece. The bottom edge weighed uncomfortably on her hipbones, in spite of the padded doublet. She felt as if a heavy hand were pressing down her chest. It was like the breathless feeling that she got when she told a lie.

"Come on and help me with the back," she said to Tamás.

Tamás was holding up a broad curving piece, turning it this way and that to see his reflection. The curve made his high cheekbones and slanting eyes spread out in a grotesque mask. Tamás stuck his tongue out at it.

"Can't you pay attention?" Phoebe took the piece out of his hands. "Where does this go?"

"Um, it's a cuisse for the top of the leg."

Actually she was surprised he remembered. He kept picking things up and putting them down, in the wrong order probably. And every time a leaf shifted in the woods he was twisting around. It gave her the creeps, the way he could swivel those ears in different directions.

"You're buckling your tassets the wrong way around," said Tamás.

Phoebe bit her lip. "I can't see them. I'm afraid to bend over."

"You should've done the legs before the body, I think."

"You know so much, why don't you help? Do these buckles."

Tamás looked up from where he squatted at her feet. "You don't have to do this, you know, Phoebe," he said with surprising fierceness.

"Yes, I do... if I'm going to do like he says and be a knight." Phoebe looked for Sir Paravent, who was a little distance away, at the opposite side of the clearing. On his silver-caparisoned charger he stood out against the dark backdrop of the forest like an emblem on a shield.

Then Phoebe frowned, looking round at the little clearing, springy green turf under her feet, the forest at her back, and the river before her slipping quietly between gravel banks. Where were the rocks they'd been sitting on, the moss, the narrow path slippery with last year's leaves?

"Tamás..." Phoebe turned right around to stare at everything. "Tamás—where is this place?"

"Why do you need to do what he says?" demanded Tamás.

"Tamás, please listen. I don't know where we are."

"This armor is much too heavy for you."

"Tamás, what are you talking about? I said everything's been changed! Can't you see that?"

"I see. I saw that before, while you were busy talking to Sir Goo-Goo Eyes."

"But what *happened* to everything?" Phoebe felt close to tears. "Where's my *house*? How could we get someplace else and not notice?"

Tamás shrugged. "How do I know? I'm only a beast."

"Tamás, don't be like that!"

He drew himself up to his full height, which was a little less than hers, because of his crooked legs. He said, "You told me you wanted to look for the other pieces of the glass, right? So where are you going to look—near the river, in the water, right? And what do you think will happen if you fall down in the middle of the water?"

"Well, I—"

"Well, you'll sink down in that armor and you'll never

get up, that's what. And that's what you should be telling to that Sir Periscope."

"Sir Peri—Sir *Paravent* said you were supposed to be my squire."

"So what?" Tamás glared at her.

He never used to act so bad tempered. Tamás never used to do anything but smile. There was something about being an animal that made him ornery, Phoebe decided. With a sigh she turned back to the pile of remaining armor. Maybe what she was already wearing would be enough for now. She still had to get up on the horse, after all.

She wondered if it was the weight of the armor that made her feel suddenly so helpless and depressed. But Paravent was right: if things were going to get all weird, she had to keep up her defenses.

"So... you can pass me up the helmet after I mount," she told Tamás.

CHAPTER VI

Sir Brillohead

Where is the Antique glory now become,
That whilome wont in women to appeare?
Where be the brave atchievements doen by some?
Where be the battels, where the shield and speare . . . ?
—*The Faerie Queene*, III, 4

IN HER IMAGINATION, Phoebe plainly saw her right leg swinging wide, a blur of bright steel, as she vaulted into the saddle. She practically felt the horse dance under her, rippling its burnished caparisons. She imagined how she would straighten her spine against its impatient movement, then stretch out her hand for the helmet with the plumes like spilt milk, for the broad shield and lance.

The way it turned out, Phoebe barely managed to lift one foot into the swaying stirrup. After ten minutes, scarlet, clanking, and gasping, she still hadn't got the other foot up from the ground. The horse kept wheeling around on her, sidling and backing its enormous armor-encased rump.

"What does it *want*?" she wailed. "Why won't it—just—stay still?"

"Try to keep calm, Phoebe," said Tamás.

"It's no good," she panted, "no—*oh*!"

The horse lurched forward, yanking her foot out of the stirrup. Phoebe toppled back. The armor crashed. One huge iron-shod hoof tore up a clump of turf beside her ear.

Tamás clung to the bridle. The horse reared up, lashing out with its forefeet, and Tamás fell away. But the instant it touched down he sprang for the head again. The noise of their trampling feet and laboring breaths moved away, toward the river.

Phoebe lay on her back, wheezing, trying feebly to rise, like an upturned beetle. Beads of sweat made sticky tracks in her hair. Then Tamás was beside her again.

"Are you okay?" she gasped as he helped her stagger to her feet. "Did it get away?"

But the horse hadn't run far. It stood with its head down, lipping grass only a stone's throw away.

"Stupid horse."

"It's not his fault, Phoebe. I think he's afraid of the armor."

"That's ridiculous!" She aimed an angry kick at the pile of leftover arms and legs lying in the grass, but Tamás bumped her aside.

"Yoy, Phoebe—you want to chase that horse all the way to New York?"

Tears gathered in the corners of her eyes. "I can't wear all this stuff. I'll never get up in the saddle."

Tamás didn't contradict her.

Phoebe breathed deep and clenched her hands. "Go get the horse," she told him. "This time, you boost, and I'll get up there if I have to take off *everything*."

Sir Paravent cantered up just in time to see her land triumphantly in the saddle. Then she had to clutch the pommel to keep from tumbling off the other side from the weight of the breastplate. That was the only piece of armor she'd been able to keep on.

Tamás danced around, bleating with concern. "Your legs, Phoebe—grip with your legs. Don't squeeze like that with your knees, you'll send him off—*keep your heels loose!*"

The big palomino bumped up and down in totally unexpected places beneath her. Phoebe was miserably conscious of presenting a ridiculous figure. What would Sir Paravent think of her now?

"Magnificent!" Paravent swept back his ostrich plumes. His face was alight with admiration.

Phoebe sat very straight in the saddle, willing the horse to stay still. She extended her hand to Tamás. She felt stiff with nervousness. "Pass up the helmet, squire."

The helmet made her head feel like it was caught in a

giant pair of pliers. If she leaned forward it hurt behind her ears. If she looked up it mashed the bridge of her nose. There were catches for securing it to something on the breastplate, but she couldn't see what.

Anyway, Phoebe decided, the helmet would stay on all right if she remembered always to sit up straight. The only problem was, she couldn't see anything when she turned her head.

"What's the matter, Phoebe? Are you okay in there?"

"I just caught my hair." She wished Tamás wouldn't always call attention to her problems. "The helmet's a little loose, is all," she said to Paravent. "It kind of shifts around."

Then Paravent said something that really surprised her. "Take out your magic glass, Belphoebe, and in its polished face admire the image of a perfect gentle knight."

"You *want* me to look in it?"

"Let it be a mirror to you," said Paravent, smiling.

"But . . . I thought you said—"

"'Never look brokenwise through the enchanted glass'? That is true, for what you see through the broken side is dark. Yet in the polished face you may behold the bright reflection of your wishéd charms."

"If that helmet doesn't fit, you should take it off," said Tamás. He stood between the two warhorses, holding the canvas-covered shield by its edges. It made him look like one of the card men in *Alice in Wonderland*.

"Let me hold it for you," urged Paravent.

"My helmet?"

"The glass."

"Oh. But I can't get it out now. It's in my pocket, under all this padding and stuff."

A small silence followed her remark. They all heard the crackle of a twig breaking someplace near at hand in the underbrush. Phoebe's horse tossed its head. She almost forgot Tamás's warnings and dug in her heels. She gripped the saddlebow instead.

Paravent stooped and hooked the shield away from Tamás. "Look, then, in the shield," he said, drawing off the canvas cover, "for all bright things give back your image."

The shield was a mirror. That is, it was not just polished steel but a real mirror, made apparently of glass. The glass had a faint rosy tinge. In it, the milky plumes of her helmet appeared pink. And the visor cast a shadow that made her eyes appear dramatically dark.

Phoebe blinked with astonishment. In the glass her image seemed more to sparkle than to blink. It looked ready for anything. It looked like Britomart the Lady Knight.

Paravent showed Phoebe how to hang the shield over her left arm so that both hands could be free to manage reins, lance, or sword. Phoebe was enchanted. Just like magic, she was a real knight.

"Now, squire, hand up the Lady's arms," instructed Paravent.

Phoebe was leaning over to check out her image in the pink shield. The helmet shifted, but she settled it easily, with one hand.

"It ought to have a liner in it," said Tamás. "Like a leather cap or something."

Phoebe laughed. He'd reminded her of that goofy leather helmet he used to wear in third grade. "Well," she said breezily, letting the visor drop down into place, "well . . . Boop-boop!"

Then, seeing his face go blank, she felt sorry. But why did he have to get all sensitive now, when that was years ago, in elementary school, for heaven's sake. Phoebe resumed a dignified expression, more suitable for a knight.

"Now, squire," she said, echoing Paravent, "hand up my arms."

Tamás gaped at her.

"Oh, come on, Tamás. Pass me the arms."

He bent slowly and picked up the two arm pieces from the discarded heap in the grass.

"Not *those* arms, duh. Pass me—"

Tamás clashed the steel arm pieces together like cymbals. They made a terrific clang. Phoebe's horse screamed and sat back on its haunches, preparing to rear. In panic she dug in her heels. The horse jolted forward.

At that moment, from all around them in the woods and underbrush arose a hideous din of shrieks and bellows, mingled with shrill whistles and rattling of gongs.

A shower of stones clattered on Paravent's armor. Tamás yelped.

Phoebe's horse bolted straight for the river. Abandoning hope of catching the reins, she clung with both hands to the saddlebow.

"Stop!" she implored the horse. "Whoa—*whoa*."

The last "whoa" came out more like a scream. In terror and frustration she actually beat on the horse's sides with her heels before she remembered that would only make it run faster.

They plunged into the river at a gallop. Water sprayed up, blinding Phoebe, soaking her pants. The horse staggered on a loose stone in the river bottom and stopped short. Phoebe was only saved from sailing off headfirst by clonking her helmet on the horse's armor-plated neck.

The big palomino squealed and bunched its haunches, ready to bolt again—then seemed to change its mind. It snorted and shifted first one heavy forefoot, then the other. Clearly it was undecided about the water.

Phoebe's eyes were full of tears. The top of her nose hurt like murder where she'd banged it inside the helmet. She tried to twist around in the saddle, to see behind her to the shore, where the others were. She could hear shouts and the clangor of gongs, and a sudden steely clash like weapons striking together.

The helmet didn't turn with her head, so she saw nothing. The horse wouldn't turn, either. She got hold of the reins and tugged to one side. The horse only braced its feet on the river bottom. She tugged harder. She jerked. The horse swung its head around suddenly to look over its shoulder at her. Its nose almost knocked her out of the saddle.

Behind her she heard Paravent's voice, raised in a war cry. He was answered with a whoop and a volley of stones; she could hear them bonking off his armor. But Tamás wasn't wearing any armor.

"Watch out!" cried Phoebe, "watch out for Tamás!"

Recklessly she took both hands from saddle and reins to drag off the helmet. She threw it into the water, where it sank in a flurry of milky plumes.

Now at last she could turn and see. In the clearing, Paravent's mounted form towered above a mob of struggling creatures. His sword rose and fell and rose again, shining in the clear light off the river.

But what were they, the creatures—men or beasts? Those were men's hands, brandishing sticks and rocks. And they wore clothing—some just rags, but others... Wasn't that one guy wearing a Wintersham Jaycees baseball jacket? And another one had on a bicycle helmet. But they had horns on their heads, too, and horny hooves for feet, and shaggy haunches. And all the while they fought, they bellowed without words, like animals.

Tamás staggered away from the fight, hands held out blindly. Blood streaked across his forehead like a bloom from Pop's Hawaiian shirt. Two of the creatures ran after him and linked their arms with his, to support him when his legs gave out.

Or else they were dragging him away. They were the enemy, weren't they? Horrible things, not even human. Except, maybe they weren't enemies to Tamás. They had legs like his.

Phoebe pleaded with the horse, "Go back—please, please, go back."

She tried to steer the horse like a bicycle, leaning to the right and squeezing only with her right knee. Her hands on the reins were fisted with anxiety.

The horse turned its head and stared doubtfully back at the bank. Then it faced around to the opposite side of the river and neighed loudly.

Another horse answered. Phoebe's head snapped around.

A strange knight mounted on a tall black charger was just approaching the water from the opposite bank. The knight's armor was all shining black as well, even to the plumes that crowned his helmet. Upright in his hand he carried a lance with a rose red pennant snapping in the breeze.

"Oh, thank God," breathed Phoebe, "help at last." Out loud she called, "Hurry—please hurry!"

She thought when the black horse crossed the river her own might turn and follow. Horses were herd animals, weren't they? Then there would be the two of them to help Sir Paravent. She looked back to where her own weapons were still lying on the ground, beside the scattered heap of armor.

When she faced round again she saw that another figure, a girl in pink, was approaching over the gentle meadow that led down to the opposite bank. The girl waved and called something, but the breeze carried her voice away. At the same time it picked up the veil from her tall pink hat and spread it out behind her like a breath of mist.

The stranger knight raised his arm with the fluttering pennant. Light off the river rippled over the black steel of his armor like a current of blue flame. He called to Phoebe, "No one may cross who does not first answer my challenge!"

"But I don't *want* to cross, can't you see? We need your help over here!"

"Nuh-uh! You have to meet my challenge." The Black Knight had a high voice, a girl's voice, with a hint of whine in it. "That's the custom; defy it if you dare. Or I—uh, I'll approve it on your carry-on corpse."

"*Carrion*, stupid," muttered Phoebe, twisting round to check on the fight. But the fight appeared to be breaking up, the savage rabble retreating into the woods with Paravent in hot pursuit. It seemed to Phoebe like a pantomime: Paravent flourishing his sword, the creatures striking grotesque attitudes of fear and dismay. In spite of all the yelling and swordplay, she couldn't spot anyone who looked seriously wounded. No bodies were left lying on the trampled ground.

"Come on, Brillohead! I'm *waiting* for thee," hollered the Black Knight.

Then Phoebe knew who it was. Jennifer Gorton, it had to be; Phoebe recognized her voice. They'd known each other since preschool, and besides, it was Jennifer who'd started that Brillohead business.

For one confused instant Phoebe thought the adventure must be over and she'd gone back to ordinary people she knew from school. But of course that was ridiculous, because why would Jennifer be wearing armor? No, the adventure was still going on, and Jennifer must be part of it.

Phoebe waved her arm over her head. "Jennifer, it's okay—it's me, Phoebe!"

Jennifer called back over the river, "I know thee, false traitor knight, Sir Brillohead of evil name!" Then she did something, leaning back in her saddle and pulling on the reins so the black horse reared up and splashed down in the water's edge. The effect was very impressive.

Jennifer could ride, of course. Also, she took acting lessons after school. Phoebe had heard she'd even done some modeling for a department store.

Meanwhile the pink girl had arrived at the riverbank

and stood lifting her skirts just clear of the water. Under the skirt she was wearing silver slippers. And she was just who Phoebe was expecting her to be, because lately Jennifer Gorton went everywhere with Staci Boyd, who used to be Phoebe's best friend. Phoebe called to her.

The breeze swept a strand of pale hair across Staci's cheek. She tucked it back, converting the gesture into a little wave.

"Oh, hi, Phoebe." Her smile panned over both Phoebe and Jennifer.

"Tell her to lay off, will you?" shouted Phoebe. "There're some people in trouble over here, Tamás Horvath and another knight, Sir Paravent. We were attacked. We need help."

Jennifer the Black Knight had been fiddling with her lance, settling it so it passed diagonally across her horse's back and pointed at Phoebe. Phoebe must not have been paying enough attention, because she was taken completely by surprise when Jennifer suddenly yelled, "Now, caitiff, fight or fly!" The black horse charged into the river.

There was nothing for Phoebe to do but duck. She threw her arms around her horse's neck and drove her heels into its ribs. The big palomino floundered sideways in the water; Jennifer's horse churned past, kicking back sheets of icy spray. Jennifer's lance missed her by inches.

The charge carried the black horse partway up the

other bank before Jennifer could check it and wheel it round to face Phoebe again.

"Jennifer, stop! Are you crazy? I surrender!"

But the black horse was already pounding down the bank, gouging up mud and gravel with its hooves. It struck the water with the sound of an avalanche.

For one very slow instant Phoebe only stared, her hands folded demurely before her on the saddlebow, the cold weight of the armor settling on her chest. Then she yelped and smacked the horse's rump, forgetting its steel casing, hurting her hand. Her heels beat a running tattoo against its ribs.

The big palomino sloshed around in a tight circle and wound up bucketing side by side with the black horse most of the way across the river. Staci gave a little scream and ran farther up the bank, to escape getting showered.

The black horse bared its teeth as Jennifer dragged at the reins. Flecks of foam showed on the horse's muzzle. Its eye gleamed white at the corner.

Now Phoebe was too close to run at with the lance.

"You creep," Jennifer hissed, "you're cheating!"

"Jennifer, time out, okay? I surrender, okay? Look, I'm not armed, I—"

Jennifer poked awkwardly at Phoebe with the barbed point of the lance, then swung it wide and tried to sweep her out of the saddle.

"Jennifer, for God's sake! You could *hurt* somebody."

The second sweep caught Phoebe on the back and made her cough. Her horse started forward, toward the center of the stream, until a dead branch riding high in the current startled it and it veered back toward Jennifer.

Phoebe might have cried, if she'd had any breath left. What would Jennifer do to her if she fell off? Would she let her surrender even then?

Phoebe might have screamed for Paravent, or even Tamás, but they had disappeared into the woods.

Jennifer was coming at her again, this time swinging the lance with two hands, like a baseball bat. Phoebe threw up her shield to protect her head. But her shield was only a mirror. A useless pink mirror. It would probably smash to bits. Phoebe was already cringing, expecting the blow.

It never fell. Something made Jennifer hesitate, the lance raised high but not completing its downward swing. *The glare,* thought Phoebe. *It must be the glare from the mirror that blinds her*. She could see the bright spot it reflected onto Jennifer's black visor. The tip of the lance wavered and came down crookedly, not doing any harm.

Then Jennifer reached up and pushed back her visor. She smiled into the mirror. She wasn't squinting. The glare didn't seem to be bothering her at all.

The sounds of the fight in the clearing had died away. The riverbank was deserted except for Staci, who sat in the grass with her arms around her knees, watching. In the silence the chuckle of the water was loud. Jennifer shifted slightly, leaning closer to the mirror. The leather of her saddle creaked.

Phoebe took a deep, ragged breath and tightened her grip on the mirror. She held it up so that Jennifer could get the full impact of the pink reflection.

"You sure look awesome in that armor," said Phoebe.

Jennifer nodded, the black plumes of her helmet bobbling like a chicken's crest. A slight, foolish smile played around the corners of her mouth.

"I mean, not everybody can really wear black, you know? You've got to have, like, a sophisticated look, you know?" Phoebe peered around the edge of the shield to see how Jennifer was taking this. She looked drunk, leaning sideways out of the saddle to gaze into the mirror. Her long lance trailed in the stream.

Phoebe said, "Anybody could tell you've had professional modeling experience; a thing like that, you can always tell."

She toed the palomino in the ribs. The surprised horse grunted softly and shifted a few paces closer to the black. Jennifer glanced up, distracted by the movement.

"You're jealous because I won the fight," she said suspiciously.

"No, no—I mean, of course you won it, but I mean, just *look* . . ." Phoebe thrust the mirror shield practically under Jennifer's nose. The two girls were almost close enough to touch now. "It's like, you just have that star thing. What I mean is, you'll probably end up in the movies or something."

Jennifer tried out a shy smile in the mirror. There didn't seem to be any limit to what she'd swallow.

Then Phoebe blushed, remembering what she'd been willing to believe herself, with her own eyes fixed on the enchanting pink vision. She plunged on.

"Actually you remind me of, uh, you know the one I mean, she just did that movie with Rick Starrett... Like, when you put your head down and kind of roll your eyes up, through your eyelashes, you look just exactly like, uh, like—"

"Like this?" murmured Jennifer.

"No, put your head down more and kind of turn, like—*this!*" Phoebe grabbed the bunch of feathers in the crest of the black helmet. She tugged down.

Jennifer was already off balance. She started to slide sideways, out of her saddle. She windmilled her arms, catching Phoebe on the ear. "Let me go-o-o!"

Phoebe was yelling, too. Jennifer kicked, and Phoebe yanked. She felt one foot slip out of its stirrup. Both horses shied away from the commotion.

And the Black Knight crashed. Jennifer's scream and an explosion of icy water filled Phoebe's eyes and ears. The palomino horse squatted back, then rose like a wave, twisting in midrise to bolt for the shore. Phoebe rolled off its back. A hoof struck her breastplate under the water. She opened her mouth and the river boiled in.

Phoebe tumbled over the stones of the river bottom. First her shoulder, then her knees bumped down; her head came up, just beneath the surface. She could see the sun shining through the glaze of running water. With a huge effort she struggled to her feet.

Water sluiced from her breastplate. Water streamed out of her hair and rained back into the river. She was standing hip deep in the stream.

The black horse stood in the meadow, beside Staci Boyd. Even from here Phoebe could see the little shivers of excitement running up its legs. The palomino must have disappeared into the woods on the other shore. But where was Jennifer Gorton?

Phoebe called her, stumbling around in the water, feeling for her with numbed hands and feet.

Staci jumped up and ran down to the water's edge. She waved and called, "Phoebe, you were terrific!"

Phoebe didn't answer. Panic had her by the throat. This was just what Tamás had warned her, you fell down in the water in your armor and you never got up. Only, it was Jennifer who was wearing all the armor.

Then she saw it, the long dark form lying under shallow water not far from where Staci stood smiling on the shore. Phoebe staggered toward it, shouting to Staci to help her, but Staci didn't seem to understand. Phoebe could see the black armor clearly now, the drowned plumes streaming like weeds.

She struggled and grunted, but she couldn't raise Jennifer out of the water. The armor must be full of water. It must weigh tons. In desperation she knelt in the stream, fumbling for the catches that fastened the black helmet on. When she felt them give she heaved the helmet up and cast it away like a stone. She was sobbing with fear that Jennifer might already be drowned, absolutely dead.

No bubbles rose to the surface. No face, alive or dead, stared back at her from the water. Jennifer simply wasn't there. With frozen fingers Phoebe unbuckled the black breastplate and pried it aside. But the armor was quite empty.

CHAPTER VII

STACI BOYD

> In lovely wise she gan that Lady greet...
> And entertaining her with curt'sies meet,
> Professt to her true friendship and affection sweet.
>
> —*The Faerie Queene*, IV, 3

STACI BURST OUT LAUGHING. "Oh, Phoebe—if you could just see your face!"

"There's nobody in there. No..." Phoebe swallowed hard to clear her clogged throat. "No body in this armor."

"Yes, I know. That's the whole joke."

"You think that's a *joke*?"

"Don't be mad." Staci made her face serious. "I don't mean like a joke, really. It's, like, a kind of a test. Nobody's supposed to come over here to the Field of Champions unless they pass the test." Staci held out her hand to help Phoebe up the bank, out of the water. "You aren't really mad, are you?"

Phoebe shook her head, partly just to clear it. She felt

too chilled to speak, too chilled to think, even. She concentrated merely on picking her feet up one after the other, as she followed Staci into the sunny meadow.

Staci said, "I thought you were just so smooth, the way you did that. And she had better armor, too."

"The armor ... got to me. Because it was empty."

Staci nodded and squeezed her hand with easy sympathy.

But now she'd got started Phoebe couldn't stop chattering. "It was just like in the story, remember? *The Faerie Queene*. That giant, what's-his-name, disappears when Prince Arthur cuts off his head—"

Staci smiled, an all-purpose hostess smile. "We'd better hurry up and get you some dry things," she said. "Your lips are blue."

"But don't you *remember*? We used to play *Faerie Queene* all the time. The giant's supposed to be pride, so when he gets put down he just kind of disappears ... like a popped balloon ... Only ..." Phoebe's voice trailed off. "That was Jennifer Gorton," she said flatly.

"Of course."

"But then—how could she just disappear like that? Where did she go?"

Staci twitched her shoulders. "Who cares? You don't want her, do you?"

Phoebe said, "I thought you liked her. I thought she was practically your best friend."

"That breeze-brain?" Staci drew her mouth up in a

pout, then let it out a bit at a time at the corners until she was laughing again. "You're my best friend, Phoebe. Since we were little kids, right?"

Phoebe eyed her thoughtfully. She seemed like the same old Staci Boyd. Maybe her hair was a little longer, more princessy. It was hard to tell under the fluttery veil. She said, "You're the pink princess, aren't you—the one in the paperweight."

"Isn't it perfect? I even have this little crown I wear, like a gold band with a pink jewel in it, here—" Staci's hands described the crown. "Like a humongous engagement ring. Then when I wear it everybody has to bow down—I don't mean *you*, Phoebe, but all the boys. I mean the knights."

They were walking up the meadow toward a bright pavilion covered in pink-and-white-striped silk. A rose-colored banner fluttered from the peak of the roof. The pavilion was shaped like a circus tent and was quite large; a dozen people could stand up and even walk around a little inside. Phoebe couldn't think how she'd missed seeing it there before.

"Are you okay?" asked Staci, catching Phoebe's arm when she stumbled over something in the grass.

"I'm freezing. And I need to know—"

"Oh, I *know*," said Staci, "but don't worry—we're about the same size, so you can wear something of mine. You're just a little taller, and bigger, you know, *here* . . ."

Phoebe twisted away from Staci to gaze back at the empty clearing across the river. She worried aloud about Tamás and Sir Paravent, what she should do.

"Don't worry about it," Staci told her. "Nothing bad's going to happen to them."

"How can you say that—nothing bad! They could be *dead* for all we know."

Staci shook her head. "You don't get it, do you? Look, Phoebe, all this"—her gesture took in the meadow, the pavilion, her own costume—"this place is, like, the Life of the Mind. It's not Real Life here, see? You don't have to get so serious about it."

"Yeah, right—don't worry, just party." Phoebe meant to sound sarcastic, but Staci laughed and bumped shoulders with her.

"Just wait," she said. "They'll show up for the tournament, I bet. Jennifer, too."

Phoebe's toe caught something that rattled in the grass. It was a long bone, dry and bleached white by the weather. There were a lot of bones, she noticed suddenly, lying around in that meadow.

Staci was telling her about the tournaments. There was a tournament almost every afternoon in the meadow, she said.

"And all the knights fight to see which one gets to be my champion. Only *you're* my champion, now, Phoebe. That'll *really* mess with their heads!"

"Staci, wait a minute. These bones—they're not *people* bones, are they?"

"Duh, Phoebe—of *course* they are. I was just telling you, wasn't I, we have these tournaments—" Staci let out a trill of laughter. "*Now* you should see your face! I *told* you it wasn't serious."

"It looks like it got pretty serious for somebody."

"Oh, chill *out*, Phoebe. You don't think these are *real*, do you? This is the Life of the Mind, remember? The bones are for *atmosphere*."

"Oh . . . I see."

"That's what I like about you, you know?" Staci confided. "You have so much imagination. I mean, most people—they can't think of anything to do unless their moms'll drive them over to the mall . . . Is that your friend?"

Phoebe wasn't exactly listening. She'd gone back to worrying about Real Life and the Life of the Mind. Staci had made them sound like actual places. Like, "You're not in Kansas anymore, Dorothy." Only she wasn't in Oz either—because that was the kicker, Staci didn't say whose Mind this was supposed to be the Life of. What if her whole adventure turned out to be just something Staci was dreaming? What if her *whole life*—

"Hey!" Staci jiggled her arm. "Snooze alarm! I said, here comes your friend."

It was Sir Paravent, down by the stream. He'd sheathed his bloody sword and taken off his helmet, so the sunlight gleamed on his smooth blond head. He looked unhurt and unhurried, his white horse placing its feet with dainty assurance as it forded the water. Behind him, meek as a lamb, trailed the palomino.

Phoebe, with Staci at her heels, raced down the meadow to meet him. Paravent swung from the saddle. He was laughing, his teeth dazzling white against his tan. He smoothed back a lock of blond hair that had fallen over his forehead.

Staci's eyes were round and her voice breathy when Phoebe introduced him. But it was Phoebe who held his deep blue gaze, Phoebe whose hand he kept in his own.

The sun on the gravel bank was warm. For the first time since she'd fallen into the water Phoebe felt her chilled muscles relaxing. Her throat stopped aching. She almost hated to ask about Tamás. She didn't want to think about anybody's problems right now.

But she had to ask. Staci had walked a few paces ahead, leading the way to the pink-and-white pavilion. Paravent bent his head down close so he could speak to Phoebe privately. She could smell the warmth on his skin, and the leather straps that fastened his breastplate, and, she thought, cologne.

"Alas," he said, "I fear some treachery was afoot. After the goat boy drove your horse away—"

"But wait—that was just a stupid trick. I mean, I don't believe he meant it like it turned out."

"What else can we believe? The trick was deliberate, and dangerous. Yet for your sake I tried to bring him back—" His hand tightened over hers. "They were too many, and he fled away before I could prevent him."

Phoebe stood still. Paravent continued on a pace or two, with her hand still in his. So when he turned to face her they seemed like two people about to perform some stiff, old-fashioned dance, a minuet, at arm's length.

She started to say, *Tamás wouldn't go with them. He was coming with us*. But when she saw the pitying expression on his face the words dried up in her throat.

Paravent said, "I am sorry, since you are grieved. He went with the others of his kind."

"They're not his kind! Tamás isn't like that really, don't you see? It's just the way he looks—"

But then she bit her lip, remembering how Paravent had explained it to her, that the image was the true self. And Tamás had acted like a goat, all right—that dumb stunt, scaring her horse, he might've got her killed on the spot, or drowned in the river. He wouldn't give her the weapons when she'd asked, either.

Suddenly she was furious with Tamás. The anger flared up all at once, bright and hot like a fire made with paper—and it lasted hardly as long. But it made her feel warmer for a little while, and stronger.

Staci had turned back when Phoebe and Paravent stopped following. Now she took Phoebe's other hand.

"I can't believe you're getting all bent out of shape about *Tamás Horvath*. You don't *like* him, do you?"

"No, I don't *like* him. It's just—well, I thought he was coming with us, is all."

Staci glanced away then, but not in time to hide the curl of her lips. "Phoebe... I don't want to be mean or anything, but *Tamás*—" She made a comic grimace, pulling down the corners of her mouth and rolling up her eyes.

Phoebe giggled. She didn't mean to, only the sound came up like a bubble, before she was aware. She thought about how the kids used to tease Tamás Horvath in elementary school. She remembered one time...

They were all out on the blacktop at recess—she, and Staci, and Tamás, with his usual little swarm of tormentors. Phoebe was doing something with chalk. She used to like to scrape the chalk stubs sideways over the blacktop, then coax patterns from the soft yellow dust with her fingers. Staci raced past, pale hair swept back against her pink knitted hat. Phoebe stretched out a hand to stop her from scattering the chalk dust. But Staci didn't stop, just reached in passing to slap Phoebe's upraised palm.

"You've got Tamás Horvath's cooties!" sang Staci.

Phoebe kept her hand stretched out stiff. Her first two fingers were stained yellow with chalk dust.

"Cooties are supposed to be head lice," she said.

Already she could feel whatever it was that was wrong with Tamás Horvath soaking into the palm of her hand, sinking roots like soft gray mold.

Staci stopped and looked at Phoebe. Her eyes were pale, pale blue. There were discs of iridescent plastic, like flakes of ice, looped into the pompon of her knitted hat. "You always know everything, don't you, Phoebe?" she said. Her voice rose clear and high, "Phoebe has To-mash Horvath's—cooo-teees!"

So Phoebe had got up and chased her. But between her shoulder blades she'd felt Tamás's eyes pressing against her skin, like gentle damp fingertips.

•

Now, once again, she had that guilty feeling about Tamás, left in the lurch, while she let herself be drawn up the sloping meadow between Staci and Sir Paravent. At the entrance to the pink-and-white pavilion Paravent took leave of the two girls. He had to tend to the horses, he said.

"Tend to them how?" said Phoebe, watching him walk away. "Where?"

"Oh, somebody'll take care of them. A servant or somebody," said Staci airily, gesturing at the empty meadow. "He's just being tactful, silly, so you can change. Come on—you can try on all my stuff."

The entrance to Staci's pavilion was looped back like a theater curtain, with heavy silken cords. Inside, Phoebe caught a glimpse of pale green Chinese carpets and silver bowls of fruit and flowers set on a low table. Above their heads the rosy banner curled and unfurled on the breeze. It bore a single word in tall silver letters: IN.

"Why does it say that?" said Phoebe. "I mean, it's the only door, right? There isn't any OUT."

"It's a *joke,* Phoebe. It's, like, the *in* place, get it? Like the *IN* place to be."

Phoebe stared up at the banner. Staring up that way made her mouth want to hang open. Then she turned for one last look down the gentle slope where butter yellow flowers bloomed amid the bones, and across the river to the woods where Tamás had disappeared with the subhuman rabble.

"Oh yeah," she said at last. "Yeah . . . I think I'm beginning to get it."

Phoebe woke up suddenly, while it was still dark. Inside the pavilion the air was close and muggy. There was a nasty taste in her mouth, and her throat felt parched.

Staci was snoring. If you could call that breathy noise a snore. She didn't use to snore, did she, back in the days when she and Phoebe had sleepovers almost every Saturday night?

She didn't use to drink wine, either. The wine had been pink, of course. Staci had poured it into long-stemmed crystal goblets.

"What's the matter?" she'd said, handing a goblet to Phoebe, "didn't you ever drink wine before?"

"My parents have it sometimes." Phoebe sipped and winced. "It's not always this sweet, is it?"

"Of course *you* know everything about it," said Staci.

Before that they'd tried on clothes and talked, mostly about boys. And about Paravent, naturally.

"Where did you *find* him?" Staci cooed.

She was standing behind Phoebe, tightening up the laces on a long, silky sea green sheath. "Suck in your stomach," she instructed.

"Do you have to make it so tight? I can hardly breathe."

"God, Phoebe, check out those curves! You look *gorgeous*."

"I feel like this is going to pop if I bend over."

"That's how it's *supposed* to look." She gave the laces one last yank before tying them off, like a tourniquet. "Tell me about *him*," Staci begged.

"Well... it was kind of a joke, really. I mean, I was looking into this piece of glass I found, like it was some kind of a crystal ball, you know? And all of a sudden this knight just *appeared* in it—I mean, it was just like when Britomart sees Artegall in Merlin's glass, remember?"

"Awesome," breathed Staci.

"Only, it turned out to be just a reflection. I mean, he was really there, just behind me, and I saw his reflection."

"But, Phoebe, that's so special, like it could be a poem or something. And besides, he's in love with you."

"Oh, I... I don't know, Staci, he—I mean, how old do you think he is?"

"Eighteen at *least*. Maybe even twenty."

"Well, see, that's what I mean. It's weird."

Besides the wine, Staci had had a picnic supper packed in a basket. It was princess food: strawberries and frosted cupcakes, dainty crustless sandwiches cut out like stars and hearts. Outside, the sky was growing overcast. Staci lit the candles in a heavy-branched candelabrum. Then she untied the silken cords to let the tent flaps down. Soon they heard the first gust of raindrops spatter against the tent.

Inside it grew warm and stuffy with the mingled odors of candle wax and damp silk, cupcake frosting, and Staci's perfume. Phoebe's hair curled as it dried, like wild grape vines. She began to feel drowsy from the heat, or from the pink wine, which tasted better after the first sips.

That was when Paravent came back. To Phoebe's astonishment, he'd changed into black jeans and a roll-neck sweater. He and Staci looked so perfect it was unreal, like movie stars, standing together with the candlelight plating their blond heads.

Even without Staci's hint Phoebe could have told that Paravent really was interested in her. But she found it hard to follow his moods. One minute he was laughing, twisting a curl of her hair around his finger. The next minute his face had gone all sulky, his eyes half-closed but burning at her from under their heavy lids. Phoebe sipped nervously at her glass of wine.

The wine brought the shadows beyond the candlelight to life. Staci got up to move the picnic things and bring out armloads of silky comforters and pillows. Past the swish of the silk Phoebe could hear the wind gusting in the trees at the bottom of the meadow.

"Tell me your name," she said to Paravent, who had stretched out beside her on a plump comforter.

He smiled at her over the brim of his wine. "I did tell you."

"No, I mean your real name. Who are you really, outside the glass?"

"Let's not think about that now. Come lie here with me."

Phoebe slid down obediently. "But what I mean is, if this's the Life of the Mind, what else have we got to do but think?"

Paravent kissed her. His lips were soft, and the kiss was as tender and wondrous as a first kiss has to be...

Except... it lasted so long... Phoebe was running out of air. She tried to sneak in a breath, but her lips made a funny smacking noise.

She sat up quickly and took another swig of her

wine. She held the goblet up to the candlelight and looked around the room through it. The bumps in the crystal pattern tickled her eyelashes. The wine slopped over the rim of her glass and splashed on Paravent's shoes.

Phoebe scrambled to her feet, saying, "Sorry, sorry." She couldn't believe she'd done such a humiliating thing. Paravent was dabbing at his shoes with a cushion. They were white loafers, with gold-tone buckles shaped like little bridle bits. *What incredibly geeky shoes.*

Phoebe groaned in the dark, remembering. She couldn't decide which had been worse, those shoes or her own utter dweebitude. But Staci had come to the rescue with a napkin left over from the picnic and the suggestion that they'd all better get some rest to be ready for the tournament tomorrow.

Now the tournament wasn't tomorrow anymore, but today. Birds were calling to each other outside. A line of bluey light showed where the tent flaps didn't quite come together.

At first Phoebe thought she'd rather skip the tournament than have to face Paravent again. Then she thought how she'd never seen a real tournament, and it must be a pretty amazing sight.

Only, those bones still worried her. She'd tried to ask Staci about them again yesterday afternoon while they were trying on clothes. But somehow they'd got off on the subject of boys.

"Why do the knights have to fight?" she'd asked. "I mean, what's the point?"

"The point is," said Staci, "I'm the princess. And I like to mess with their heads."

"But *why* do you like to? How can you have a relationship with somebody if you're always messing with his head? He'll never feel comfortable."

"It's because I don't *want* them to feel comfortable. Listen, Phoebe—you know, once guys get comfortable, pretty soon they'll want to be the boss. Then they'll start telling *you* what to do. I want to keep them wondering all the time."

Phoebe said, "It just doesn't seem like much of a friendship."

And Staci said, "You really are so funny and sweet, Phoebe. That's why I'm glad you're my champion."

Phoebe rolled over uneasily in her nest of comforters. Yesterday she'd been thinking about the boys, and the bones. Now something else about that remark struck her unpleasantly. She sat bolt upright, her eyes wide open. Staci's *champion! Oh, my God, does that mean I have to fight all the others? Why didn't she* tell *me? Why didn't I ask her what she meant?*

The sudden change of position made her brains whirl. Her stomach felt squashy. She pressed her forehead to her knees and moaned, "I want to be sick."

And what would happen to her at the tournament if

she lost? *When* she lost—there could hardly be any *if* about it. Would she disappear like Jennifer—like a popped balloon?

"Why is this happening to me?" Phoebe cried out loud. Near her in the dark, Staci stirred in her sleep and sighed.

Phoebe decided to run away. She wouldn't fight. She didn't care what Staci thought about her. Staci could have some dumb boy for her champion—or Jennifer Gorton, if Jennifer came back for the tournament like Staci said she would.

Phoebe almost laughed when she thought how jealous she used to be of Jennifer. Poor Jennifer. The truth was, she was a dim bulb, in spite of the riding, and the acting lessons, and the modeling. *There must be something about jealousy,* Phoebe thought, *that makes you build people up, see them as more impressive than they are. You just create your own enemies out of thin air.*

Then Phoebe made a noise like a puppy yip and had to stuff her fingers into her mouth and bite them to keep from waking Staci.

Because she realized now why Jennifer had disappeared. The Black Knight was never the real Jennifer Gorton. It was created by Phoebe's jealousy, like the giant that turned out to be just air in Spenser's poem. Now Phoebe had pushed Jennifer aside so she could take her place with Staci in the IN crowd. Meanwhile, Tamás was left behind on the other side of the river with the subhuman types, the geeks. This was the Life of Phoebe's own Mind.

That was the reason all these things were happening to her. They always had been happening. What had changed was the way she was seeing them. Ever since she'd looked through the magic glass things had started to look like what they really meant. It was like the way poetry worked. Pop had told her imagination shows you reality.

What I need now, thought Phoebe, *is the footnotes, so I can understand everything. And I need my shoes.*

She was still wearing the green silk gown, which rucked up under her arms and felt clammy from sweating under the comforters. She had no idea what Staci had done with her real clothes.

Maybe Paravent had taken them. Phoebe thought she remembered he'd asked last night where she'd put her stuff. Probably he was worried she'd left the piece of glass in her pocket.

But he should have realized she wouldn't be so careless. No, she'd taken it out of her pocket and slipped it into the toe of her shoe, which was under that low table with the candles on it. She'd stuck her shoes there because they embarrassed her, a pair of bulgy old size-eight Docksiders, next to Staci's narrow silver slippers.

Phoebe rose cautiously and groped her way to the table. The shoes were where she'd left them, with the piece of glass. She clutched it gratefully, loving its coolness in her sticky palm.

On top of the table was a massive dome-lidded chest she certainly hadn't seen the night before. Maybe her clothes were in there. She opened the chest slowly, trying not to let the latches clank.

Inside, her fingers told her, was another suit of armor.

For a moment she only stood in front of the open chest, listening to the happy riot of the birds outside. She had a feeling under her ribs like she'd swallowed one of the birds. Then she went and drew back one flap of the tent and tied it with the cord.

Sweet air flowed into the pavilion, along with enough light to see the armor clearly. It looked like another complete suit, with a sword belt tucked in beside it. On a pink velvet cushion reposed the helmet. It had a cheese-grater visor, like the one she'd thrown away, and plumes the color of spilt milk. Phoebe shuddered.

But there was more, a slashed and padded arming doublet and a pair of matching knee-length drawers. Phoebe stripped off her tight green sheath and quickly pulled on the padded clothes. They fit comfortably and were easy to move in, like sweats.

Around her waist she knotted one of the silken cords from the tent flaps. Because you never knew, even in the Life of the Mind a piece of rope might come in handy.

Her toe bumped a silver bowl of fruit that someone had moved off the table to make room for the big chest.

Peaches rolled everywhere. They were too soft to pack, so Phoebe ate as many as she could. They helped a little to settle her stomach. Some apples and pears she stuffed into the lining of her doublet, through the slashes.

Then she was ready to go. But at the entryway of the IN pavilion she paused to look back at her friend. Staci's shoulder was bare, her pale hair tangled in the hollow of her neck. Her hand lay palm up, fingers gently curled, on the pillow. Phoebe went in again, just for a minute, to draw up the silky comforter.

She bent down and touched Staci's hand softly, not meaning to wake her. "Now you have Tamás Horvath's cooties," Phoebe whispered.

CHAPTER VIII

QUEEN EVERGREEN

Upon his hands & feete he crept full light,
And like a Gote emongst the Gotes did rush.
—*The Faerie Queene*, III, 10

A MIST LAY OVER THE RIVER, blotting Phoebe's view of the other side. As the light grew the mist thinned and turned golden. Then she could make out the woods—first the pale spines of beeches, then dark evergreens crowning the ridge where she thought River Road used to be. A haze of tender green followed the line of the water.

Phoebe was sorry she'd lost her socks. The meadow grass was wet and stung her ankles. Still, as the mist lifted she felt her spirits rise also. She marched down to the water's edge with barely a glance at the drowned black armor. But the water itself was daunting, bright as ice—just standing beside it made her skin come up in goose bumps sharp as pinches.

She'd have to take off her shoes and her warm quilted pants, or they'd be soaked for the rest of the day. Phoebe's toes curled with embarrassment. What would Paravent think if he saw her sloshing around in her underpants? She still felt haunted by his look of disgust when the wine spilled on his white shoes.

Phoebe shut her eyes against this image, but immediately another face came to mind: Tamás, with his chin cocked up, saying proudly, "Magyars are men of Hungary, not goats." Wasn't it funny, she'd never asked Tamás where his family came from. She wondered if anybody at school knew.

Phoebe took a deep breath and sat down to take off her shoes. Even though the water was freezing and it meant taking off her pants right outside, where anybody might see, the other side was where Tamás had disappeared. If she didn't go back he would haunt her forever.

By the time she stepped gingerly up on the stones of the opposite bank she'd stopped thinking about anything but the breathtaking cold of the river. She stuffed her feet into her shoes and jumped around, flapping her arms and making a sort of caveman sound, "*Hunh—hhunhg,*" trying to get dry.

Until, suddenly, she remembered the fight in the clearing. The wordless cries and beastlike faces—*oh, God, those creatures might still be lurking around here.*

"Well, so what?" she said, her voice sounding puny in

her ears. If she was going to find Tamás, she'd have to start by finding his captors. Unless they found her first. Phoebe pulled her pants on over her wet skin.

One plan might be to follow that forest trail where she'd first seen Sir Paravent. It made sense to her that if this country was somehow made up out of her own mind, that trail must be like the river path that led to the Steephill Road bridge. Hadn't she and Tamás been sitting right by the path when Paravent showed up and everything began to look different? So, if she followed the trail upstream, eventually she'd come to a bridge, and on the other side would be Mr. Barnes's store. Archimago's castle.

There her imagination came to a full stop. She pulled her piece of glass from its nest in the wadding of her arming doublet and spent some time looking at it, how the light fell down inside the glass and seemed to stay. She ran her thumb over the edges of the broken side, wishing it weren't dangerous to look through. Phoebe sighed and knuckled her eyes and put the glass away again.

The forest trail was easy to find, where it curved close to the water. Once among the trees Phoebe trod stealthily and peered hard at every clump of brush.

In real life most of the land along this side of the river belonged to some people called Norris. An architect had come from New York to build them a big new house near the corner of River Road and Steephill, but most of the time they were away, in the city. Mrs. Horvath rented a little tumble-down place that used to be the farmhands' bunkhouse before the Norrises bought the property. The river path cut pretty near Tamás's house.

Was it possible that Tamás had simply gone home? But how could he, if he was a captive? *If* he was—Paravent had talked like he'd gone with those creatures willingly.

The trail led through a stand of young spruce trees that crowded thick and prickly beside the way. As she walked Phoebe pinched off pale green spruce tips and shredded them in her fingers.

She wondered where Paravent had gone after he left the pavilion last night. What would he think when he got up this morning; would he be disappointed she'd gone on without him? Would he come after her? As long as she stayed on this trail Paravent could surely guess where to find her.

Then should she wait for him? It might be a long wait, if he was going to be in the tournament. But Paravent didn't care about being Staci's champion, did he? He'd seemed so eager, yesterday, to join in the quest with Phoebe.

Maybe she was making too much of last night's embarrassment. Phoebe threw away the sprig of evergreen she'd been worrying in her fingers. Probably she was acting incredibly stupid, starting on the quest without the knight in shining armor. After all, what help would Tamás be, even if she succeeded in finding him?

Somewhere nearby a dry stick snapped, and Phoebe froze in her tracks. Then from a branch above her head a jay shrieked. A twig came rattling down. The bird vanished in a snap of blue.

Phoebe sighed with relief. Not that she meant to let those freaky creatures scare her. Really, they had nothing to do with her. No, it was Tamás they'd been after, right from the start. They'd come to claim him for Geek-land, just like Staci had tried to make her and Paravent join the IN crowd. Only, the thing was, people who were really geeky did tend to give you the creeps.

But maybe not when you got to know them. Like she'd been getting to know Tamás. What kind of life did Tamás have in his mind, she wondered. Was it like getting left outside all night in the cold and rain? He'd been out two nights in a row now. And somebody'd hit him during the fight; she'd seen the blood on his face. Phoebe wondered suddenly how Tamás had got his nose broken. Did other kids do that to him?

Then the jay shrieked again from a thicket of young spruce, and this time Phoebe heard a shrill answering note, like a pennywhistle.

Two creatures crashed through the thicket onto the path before her. A thin scream forced itself up Phoebe's throat, but she clamped her hand over it. Oh, God, what would they do—would they hit her? She ordered herself to keep calm. *Say something calm and friendly.* Phoebe arranged her lips into a smile. She could feel the smile drying against her teeth.

The creatures didn't speak. They were definitely the same kind that had grabbed Tamás. She saw they wore remnants of human clothing, but their legs were rough haired and backward bending, goat legs, with goat-hooved feet. Sharp horns jutted from their foreheads, which were low and sloping like in pictures of cavemen.

But somehow, seen up close, they looked more human, or at least less frightful, than her imagination had painted them the day before. They had hands and walked upright on two legs, the same as people. And they were young, practically kids. They stood shoulder-to-shoulder and gazed at Phoebe with mild, blank expressions.

These guys were definitely geeks. One of them was dressed in the grayed remains of a short-sleeved button-down shirt. Several pens were clipped to the pocket. He even wore glasses, with square gray plastic frames mended at one corner with masking tape. In his hand he carried a plastic soprano recorder, the kind that make a really ear-splitting squeal when they're overblown.

The other geek was thick and squat. He wore only a T-shirt that rode up over his furry stomach. His shirtfront looked like he'd been eating pizza.

Phoebe finally said, "Uh, hi." But there was something

wrong with her throat; maybe the scream was still stuck in there. The sound came out like a little bleat. She half raised her hand in a limp salute.

Pizza-Mess bleated back. Then, as if they'd been suddenly released from a spell of silence, they both rushed toward her, *bah*-ing and grunting and reaching out their hands. Pen-Pocket cut loose with a cheek-popping blast on his recorder. Pizza-Mess bounded forward with a rolling gait like an ape's; but he reared up when he reached Phoebe, and grabbed her hand. His hand was hot and damp, and rough across the knuckles from the way he walked.

Phoebe's nerve snapped. Tearing her hand away, she turned to flee. In the blindness of her panic she actually ran down another of the geeks, who'd been standing unnoticed on the path behind her.

The creature squeaked and fell over. It was a fat girl in a skimpy party dress, who lay on her back with her little goat feet up in the air like a Thanksgiving turkey. There were two others beside her, a skinny girl and a very freckled boy with a runny nose and a wide, wet grin.

Phoebe stood frozen in midflight, one hand stretched out before her as if she'd been playing a game of statues. The skinny girl came forward and took the outstretched hand in a limp but unexpectedly clingy clasp. She was so thin Phoebe could see the ridges on her windpipe above her round white collar. The fur on her goat legs wasn't coarse and curly like the others', but lank and soft looking, like a wet cat.

Meanwhile the little fat girl had rolled to her feet. Phoebe forced herself to say, "I'm sorry," though the words came out hardly more than a croak. The girl answered with a nicker that made her short upper lip quiver. She wore glasses so thick her moist brown eyes looked like melted chocolate.

Then the freckled boy removed his finger from his nose and took Phoebe's other hand. That made Pizza-Mess frown, but at a squeal from the plastic recorder they all joined hands in a line. Led by the shrilling of the recorder, they began to dance raggedly up the path.

Phoebe straggled along with them. She tried to ask where they were going, or if they'd seen Tamás, but the geeks only grinned and nodded and *bah*-ed. After ten minutes of frisking and stumbling through the woods, she was too breathless to ask any more.

Suddenly the geeks let go of her hands. The dance stopped. All around her they were jumping up and down, clapping their hands in excitement like little kids at a birthday party.

They'd come to a broad lawn, soft underfoot, dotted with clumps of young spruce and laurel. Across the lawn there actually was a table set for a birthday party, with bunches of paper streamers and balloons. Half a dozen children in paper party hats clustered around the birthday girl seated at the head of the table.

Phoebe's blood began to roar in her ears. She toppled over onto the lawn and lay there facedown, tasting the grass.

The children were tall as trees. They were giants.

Phoebe thought about crying, but it seemed somehow like a lot of work. After a few minutes the little fat girl geek came and prodded her ribs with the point of a tiny hoof. She helped Phoebe to stand up again and held her hand as, together with the rest of the geeks, they advanced shyly on the birthday party.

Phoebe walked with her eyes fixed straight ahead, on the cluster of colored balloons. The balloons were printed with white letters:

HAPPY BIRTHDAY EVERY DAY
QUEEN EVERGREEN

At the edges of her vision the giants loomed like thunderheads towering above the horizon. Their happy voices boomed among the treetops.

The little geeks gathered by the chair of the birthday girl—was that Queen Evergreen? They gazed wistfully up at the party until the giant swung her feet and sent them scurrying to the shelter of a table leg. Phoebe saw that the table rested on four young trees with branches trimmed back but roots still growing in the ground.

She peered around the table leg at the legs of the Queen. Queen Evergreen was wearing a short baby-doll-style party dress with a ruffle around the hem. Her legs were very hairy; her kneecaps were the size of trash-can lids. Her giant feet flexed. She was tilting back in her chair. Phoebe could see her face now, like the moon rising above the table's edge. She wore a crown of crumpled gilt paper.

"Eew! Ugh!" thundered the Queen. "I smell something."

"It's *them*. Who let *them* come here?" Phoebe thought that came from a boy giant sitting on the Queen's far side. She could see his Reeboks on the chair rungs, like bears roosting in the limbs of a tree. She shuddered, grateful not to be underneath.

A rumble of other voices joined in. She had trouble hearing what they said. The voices were too loud; her ears couldn't make sense of that much sound.

A block of ice came hurtling over the edge of the table and shattered near Phoebe. A fragment stung her cheek.

"Cut that out or I'll *kill* you," bellowed the Queen. "I'll throw you in jail and make you eat snot sandwiches!"

"Snot sandwiches with *mustard*," a girl's voice blared over the hubbub of other sounds.

"I'm the birthday girl and I'm the Queen and I can do it if I want," chanted Queen Evergreen. Two blond braids like rolled-up carpets swung down behind her chair. "It's time to sing," she announced.

Around the table the giants scraped back their chairs and straggled to their feet. Phoebe cringed against the table leg. But the geeks had begun to climb it.

"Be careful. Are you crazy?" she cried, but the geeks

didn't listen. They hauled themselves up, scraping off buttons and clutching for handholds among the stubs of branches. Their goat feet scrabbled against the bark.

Staring up after them, Phoebe saw a face peering over the edge of the table. It was a little face, with goatish horns and ears. Little hands reached down to help the struggling geeks around the edge to the tabletop. The fat girl, last in line, had arms too short to reach. She hung jackknifed over the topmost branch, whimpering for help.

A giant hand fumbled under the tabletop. It plucked the girl off by the back of her dress. For a moment she dangled in midair, flapping and gaping like a very slow fish. Then she was deposited on the table, out of Phoebe's view.

"Now I want to *sing*," said the Queen.

"Wait. We missed one." The voice and the great mass came down together, contracting out of the sky like a building collapsing.

Phoebe fell flat on the grass with her hands over her head, but it was too late—the giant fingers were clamping around her ribs. Then all the breath that didn't get squeezed out right away got left behind on the ground as Phoebe felt herself hoisted up into the air.

Before her like a cliff wall was a face, and most especially a mouth that gaped vast and wet. There were teeth in there that could snap her arms and legs and grind and crush them—oh, God—

But the mouth was smiling. "Look, it's a new one," it

said, ruffling Phoebe's hair with warm, lemonade-scented gusts.

"Help! Stop!" gasped Phoebe. But the words came out choked: "*Uhp! Urp!*"

"Cat-box breath!" said the giant boy cheerfully. He opened his hand and Phoebe dropped heavily onto the table, where she crawled around on hands and knees like a bug. She tried not to cry, but her nose dripped anyway.

Above her head the Queen said, "Lookit that hair. I'm going to call it Brillohead."

"I want to call it Fart Face," said the boy. "I saw it first."

"Butt out, butt breath. I'm the Queen, and I'm the birthday girl, and I can do what I want."

Phoebe struggled to her feet. To steady herself she set her hand on the rim of a paper cup half-filled with blocks of ice. She didn't touch the place where the rim was wet and marked with big dents from giant teeth. She said, "My name is Phoebe, and I am not an *it*."

The Queen leaned across the table to get a better look. One braid slid forward from her shoulder and smacked Phoebe in the chest, making her stagger.

"Did it talk?" asked Queen Evergreen.

"Goats don't say anything," said the boy.

Who are you calling a goat? Phoebe meant to say, but the words came out in a rush and wrong. She was starting to bleat like a geek. In sudden terror she looked down at her feet. They looked the same as always.

Maybe all the geeks looked okay to themselves. Maybe they all talked sense to themselves, too.

The boy had lost interest anyway and joined another boy across the table, trying to stab the floating balloons with cake forks. The Queen was swiping roses off the cake and licking her fingers.

The cake was three layered and came up to Phoebe's chin. It smelled overpoweringly of sugar. Creme filling oozed out between the layers. Phoebe's stomach growled fiercely.

She looked up around the circle of huge, happy faces. She saw chins, mostly, and slabs of moist lower lip. Pink cheeks sloped up to eyes she couldn't see behind the curve of the cheeks. She could look up noses.

At the center of the table were the geeks. There were several she hadn't seen before; they must have been on the table already. All of them were picking over a heap of what looked like musical instruments. Pizza-Mess clutched a Mickey Mouse ukulele. The little fat girl geek was trying to blow on a military bugle. Her cheeks bulged crimson, but all she produced was a stifled squeak.

A balloon exploded. All the geeks, including Phoebe, flinched and ducked. The giant boy laughed so hard a fragment of wet cake flew out of his mouth and landed on Phoebe's shoe. She stood staring at it dully until the skinny girl came over and thrust an instrument into her hands.

It was a big black bassoon, like a double fold of ebony intestine, gleaming with silver keys.

"I never played one of these before," said Phoebe.

The girl wasn't listening. She had a fussy way of doing things, plucking at Phoebe's sleeve, breathing in her face.

"See, I play the clarinet," Phoebe told her. "It's got a different kind of a mouthpiece. This's got a double reed—"

But the skinny girl was shooing her into line with the rest of the geeks.

The rest of the geeks. The phrase formed in Phoebe's mind and stayed there like the dark cloud that sweeps over an April morning, the cloud that says: The picnic will be canceled. *The rest of the geeks*. Hadn't she always known—since that day Staci slapped her hand on the playground, crying, "You've got Tamás Horvath's cooties!"—she was indelibly marked. Brillohead. Van der Klutz. Stained with contagion. Anybody who looked at her could tell.

The line of geeks wavered and regrouped as more instruments joined the haphazard band, ready to serenade Queen Evergreen. Phoebe found herself staring at a dark-haired boy with a flute at the end of the row.

When he turned his head she saw he was Tamás Horvath.

CHAPTER IX

ANGELINA

> ... But that faire one,
> That in the midst was placéd paravaunt,
> Was she to whom that shepheard pypt alone,
> That made him pipe so merrily, as never none.
>
> —*The Faerie Queene*, VI, 10

TAMÁS WAS HOLDING THE FLUTE all wrong, like a stick he meant to break over his knee. It was an antique-looking wooden orchestra flute with silver keys. When Phoebe called to him he looked up, but his glassy eyes slid past her without a flicker of recognition.

"Oh, thank God you're okay," she cried, though there was a purplish gash over his brow that would surely leave a scar. He was going to end up looking like a real tough, with his broken nose and scar. Or he would if he didn't have that idiot smile.

Tamás raised the flute to his lips and blew a hollow

note. All the geeks were struggling with their instruments: squeak, blat, hoot. No wonder he didn't hear her. Phoebe flapped her hand wildly.

"Tamás! It's *me*, Phoebe!"

Why did he keep smiling like that, like a total dweeb? He didn't need to smile at *her*. Because Phoebe was beginning to understand Tamás's smile. It was his brand of armor, like hers had been hiding out, and pretending, and lies.

Before she could speak to him again Queen Evergreen started beating a great flat cake server against the edge of the table. It made a noise like backstage thunder and sent panic waves through the huddled geeks.

The geeks launched into a jumbled fanfare on their instruments. The slide of a trombone shoved Phoebe in the back. She stumbled out of the herd and immediately felt horribly exposed on the wide smooth tabletop.

But the giants didn't notice her. The Queen was bellowing for her birthday song. The other giants had placed their hands more or less over their hearts, except for one who was giving the girl beside him rabbit ears. There was some elbowing and thunderous giggling. Then they began to sing—

"HAPPY BIRTHDAY DEAR QUEEN—"

The geeks scrambled to catch up with their musical accompaniment. Phoebe found a neck strap attached to her bassoon. She slipped it on over her head as if she meant to play, but meanwhile she was sidling behind the others, toward Tamás.

"OUR QUEEN E-*VER*-GREEN!" roared the giants.

Tamás was still wearing Phoebe's jean jacket. She tugged on the sleeve.

"Hey—I've been looking for you."

Tamás stared straight ahead and said nothing.

"EVERY DAY YOU GROW TALLER,

BECAUSE YOU'RE NEVER GROWN-UP ENOUGH!"

The giants sang the whole song over four or five times more, each time a little louder, until the whole grassy clearing among the spruce trees seemed solid with the din, like a bowl of quivery pudding.

"Hey! I got here!" said Phoebe, close to Tamás's ear.

Tamás raised the flute to his eye, grinning down the length of it, waggling one of the keys.

"Listen, I'm sorry I couldn't come right away. I met some people ..." It was frustrating to talk like this, at the side of Tamás's head. Couldn't he at least look at her?

"Tamás, *please* talk to me. Nobody'll talk to me here. They act like I'm just *bah*-ing or something, and I *can't bear it*—" Phoebe could hear her voice rising, humiliatingly out of control.

The skinny girl came over and nudged her arm. Her face wore a worried frown that wrinkled oddly around the nubs of her horns. She gestured to Phoebe's bassoon.

They were all supposed to be playing music for the Queen.

Phoebe clamped her lips around the mouthpiece and managed to produce a lugubrious honk. Big hot tears rolled down her cheeks.

Tamás was staring up at the balloons now. At least he wasn't grinning anymore.

"Tamás, you really can hear me, can't you? Listen... Listen, I'm sorry if I—ever did anything—teased you or anything... I was just... I was immature, okay? I didn't know how it felt."

Did he shrug his shoulders? Was that supposed to be an answer?

"Please—" she began, but then abruptly she was furious. "Who do you think you're kidding?" she shouted at him. "You could've killed me—you *knew* I couldn't handle that horse! So now you want me to get down on my knees and kiss your woolly toes? Well, you're just full of it, Tamás Horvath! *You're nothing but a baby goat!*"

For a moment Tamás turned to look at her. The corners of his mouth were tight, but there was no trace of his usual glassy grin. Somehow Phoebe's anger had set them, for once, eye-to-eye. Then Tamás looked away.

"Don't talk anymore now," he said, barely above his breath. "It's too dangerous here." He turned his attention back to the flute and began twisting the head joint around like he really knew what he was doing.

Phoebe worked out "Happy Birthday to You" on the bassoon. It sounded like the lament of a wounded goose.

But all the time she was thinking about Tamás. Tamás acted like a kid and got changed into a baby goat. Wasn't that how Paravent explained it, that the image in the glass was your true self? But how could anybody's true self be just one image? Real people kept changing every minute. Like, say you were immature—you could grow up, couldn't you?

Mechanically, she began another round of "Happy Birthday." The double reed buzzed and tickled her teeth. She hardly noticed when the giants stopped singing.

Even the geeks, she thought. In real life they'd be whole people, not just Fat Girl or Nerdy Guy or whatever. Other kids—kids like these dumbbell giants—might treat them like subhumans, but that wasn't the way they felt inside.

Then Phoebe almost blew out her eardrums, because a giant finger was stuck down the bell of her bassoon, blocking the passage of air. She looked up, stupid with surprise, like a possum caught in the glare of approaching headlights.

The giant boy's eyes were pale and bright. Each one held a small pool of light. *Like fishbowls*, Phoebe thought, fascinated.

The boy waggled his finger in the bassoon. Phoebe, with the reed still in her mouth, wagged her head. Then she jerked away—but he must have pushed at the same time, because the mouthpiece banged against her lip. Phoebe tasted blood.

The boy removed his finger from the bassoon. Without taking his eyes off Phoebe, he slid his hand across the table to pick up a plastic fork. It was the size of a small leaf rake. Phoebe watched him. He had ears that stuck out from the sides of his head and seemed to glow with the light behind them. The tip of his nose was pink. He was smiling a little, breathing through his mouth the way small children do when they concentrate.

And still she only watched—though fear was roaring in her ears, and every beat of her blood yelled, *Run! Hide!*

The giant hand moved suddenly. The fork sailed up, stabbed down. Phoebe screamed. The fork raked through her hair. Dragged up by its roots, she teetered on tiptoe, yelling at the boy to stop, help, let go, *please*.

The boy twisted the fork. He must have made some joke, because all around her giant laughter fell like rocks out of the sky.

Phoebe clutched at the hard tines, letting her knees sag so the fork might bend. The bassoon swung painfully from her neck. She felt her eyes, blurry with tears, stretch open wider and wider. All around her the noise of giants shouting and howling grew louder and louder.

So at first when she heard the music, a ripple of sweet

notes, she didn't think it was real. She accepted it like anything else that might happen as she slipped off the edge of consciousness into dream, or nightmare.

Just then the fork cracked. Her hair slipped free, and she pitched forward, ramming the bassoon against her breastbone. The pain made her grunt and rock on her knees, cradling the bassoon to her chest.

Above her bowed head the music took flight, a cloud of butterfly arpeggios. Phoebe looked up and breathed a small mew of wonder. It was Tamás. *Tamás* was playing the flute.

All around the table the hubbub of giant voices ground to silence. Giant faces sagged in soft O's of surprise. The giant boy's hands slipped away from Phoebe, off the table, like a wave drawn down the beach to the sea.

Tamás paused for a moment to glance at her. "This is where the piano comes in," he said. "It's a sonata." He raised the flute to his lips again.

And it was true; she could hear how the flute raced an imaginary piano. Then it settled into a swaying, rollicking melody in a minor key. It was like the river shining over small stones. Every now and then Tamás would lower the flute and mumble to himself, nodding his head with jerky emphasis to the sound of the unseen piano. How many times had she seen him doing that, at the bus stop, in some corner of the schoolyard, and thought he looked an absolute idiot? But really he was like some wild faun god of the river and woods.

The second movement of the sonata was slower, tinged with delicious melancholy. Phoebe thought about standing on the bridge, watching the water slip below her, deep and green. One of the geeks sighed. Another scratched. The giants shifted their heavy feet under the table.

Queen Evergreen leaned forward, chin on hands. Her eyes were dreamy. Her elbows thumped the table.

The thump made the music skip. Tamás recovered quickly, launching into a brilliant allegro section. But the damage was already done.

One time at band practice in sixth grade, Harley Watson dropped the bass drum while he was trying to fasten it to its marching harness. The drum rolled right across the gym floor, reverberating in the sudden hush of Mrs. Gorton's gathering wrath. It was like that now.

The Queen grinned. A roll of giggles rumbled down the table. At the opposite end another giant girl thumped her elbows, deliberately this time. When the music didn't skip, she shoved the table with the heel of her hand. Tamás staggered.

The Queen shoved back. Tamás fell on his face, his body humped protectively over his instrument. Queen Evergreen reached out and hauled him to his feet. "Play," she commanded.

Tamás played. The giant boy, Phoebe's tormentor, was

the next to join the fun. He rapped on the table with the butt of the broken fork until the music fell apart and Tamás was forced to prance about on his little goat feet to stay upright.

The other geeks were rocking and clutching each other. As the table shuddered they seemed to dance the cha-cha. The little fat girl lost her balance and rolled, rump over roses, down the table until she fetched up in a smear of chocolate icing. There she sat, red faced, holding her ruined party skirt out stiffly by the hem while the giants roared like lions for her blood. But really they were only laughing at the fun.

A dollop of cake flipped through the air past Phoebe. Tamás was playing again, shakily; but the next wad of food struck him on the shoulder, half spinning him around.

"*Cut it out, you guys!*" Queen Evergreen pounded the table with her fists.

The giant boys were shooting ice cubes across the table now. Two giant girls harrassed geeks with blasts from their party blowers. Tamás crouched, heedless of the missiles that rained on him from all sides. He was disassembling his flute, stowing the sections in the pockets of the Hawaiian shirt.

Phoebe began to crawl on hands and knees, dragging the bassoon, toward the edge of the table. *Please, God, don't let them notice,* she prayed as she swung her legs over the side, groping with her toes for the first stubby branch on the way down. With her feet on the branch and her knuckles turning white on the table edge, she looked back at Tamás.

He was wrapping the head joint of the flute in some waxed paper left over from the sandwiches she'd made the day before. Queen Evergreen, fingers stuffed in her mouth to stop the giggles, held a paper cup poised over his bent head. He was going to get drenched.

If there was ice in there it could brain him! Phoebe's mouth gaped, but she didn't shout a warning. What good would that do?

Queen Evergreen waved the cup in the air, prolonging the joke. Some other giants had noticed now. They were nudging each other, hushing their noise.

Phoebe slid down the table leg like a fireman, just scraping her palms on the limbs as they flashed by. With her feet inches from the bottom, she almost hanged herself when the bassoon strap snagged—then snapped. Phoebe rolled on the ground, coughing.

The bassoon ... She crawled over to where it lay, under the Queen's chair.

There Phoebe was forced to pause and ease her rasping breath. *Breathe* out. *Count to three*. *Breathe* in. *Lift your rib cage!*

It was Althea's voice she heard in her mind. *Beautiful breath makes beautiful sound*, she'd say.

Phoebe felt a sudden pang of homesickness. But she couldn't think about that now. Tamás was in danger.

Phoebe set the bassoon to her lips and took a full breath, summoning all the power of heart and lungs to the top of her throat. She blew. The bassoon gave forth a sonorous, deep, vibrato blat.

Above her at the table of the giants there was sudden silence. Then big giggles, then uproar.

"Pee-yew! It's you!"

"I did *not*!"

Phoebe barely had time to dodge when the Queen jumped to her feet.

"Gas attack! Gas attack!" howled the boy, dancing his mammoth Reeboks.

"I DIDN'T! IT WAS HIM!"

Phoebe left the bassoon on the ground and set off in a crouching dash toward a clump of early-blooming laurels. A stream of escaping geeks was already dropping over the side of the table. From her hiding place among the laurels, Phoebe watched them scurry past. The little fat girl paused to hold out a hand to Phoebe. Phoebe took the hand, but when the girl tried to pull her up she shook her head. She pointed back at the giants' table, where Tamás, last of the geeks, was just dangling his legs over the edge.

"Good-bye," said Phoebe, letting go the sticky little hand.

The girl fluttered her lips. Her eyes dropped away

from Phoebe's. "Good-bye," she whispered hoarsely. Then she scampered away after the others.

Queen Evergreen was having a temper tantrum. Her chair fell backward and bounced stupendously. "*I am the birthday girl!*" she bawled.

"Beans, beans, the musical fruit!" chanted the giants.

"I'LL NEVER INVITE YOU AGAIN!"

"The more you eat, the more you toot!"

The Queen seized her end of the table and banged it up and down. Tamás fell the rest of the way off the table leg. But he was all right. He got up, patting at his pockets to check the flute, and staring all around.

"*The more you toot, the better you feel!*"

Phoebe hissed, "Tamás! Over here."

He started forward just in time. The Queen, aided by eager partygoers, was tipping the table right over. Small things slid off first, instruments and blocks of ice, forks sailing like javelins into the grass. Then the cake began a stately avalanche. But by that time the giants were making so much noise that Phoebe and Tamás, running for the cover of the woods, didn't hear it hit the ground.

It was hard to keep pace with Tamás. Phoebe's legs were longer, but Tamás went in big, uneven bounds, like a mountain goat. They stopped sometimes to clutch their sides and pant, and once just to let out the gusts of laughter that had built up like silly gas.

At last Phoebe dropped down on a bank of dry ferns beside the trail. She could feel the dampness of the ground seeping up through the ferns, but she was too beat to care.

"Do you think they followed?" she asked Tamás.

"No. Kids like that—they'll chase if they see you're running, but not for long. They know they can always catch you some other time. Or they catch somebody else." He fingered the crook in his nose absently. The jean jacket was a mess of chocolate smears and soaked in lemonade. It had dried as they ran, but then it got stiff. Tamás's hair stuck up in spikes. He smelled deliciously of sweet lemonade. Phoebe's stomach growled.

"Do you want an apple?" she asked, remembering the fruit she'd stashed in the lining of her arming doublet. By the time she'd worked them out of the slashes the pears looked pretty beat up.

"They're sweeter when they're brown," said Tamás.

He ate all three pears, plus an apple. Phoebe ate two apples in big random bites while she filled him in on the story of Staci and the pink pavilion.

"So what happened to Lassie?" said Tamás.

"Who?"

"The horse."

"Oh . . . I left him with Sir Paravent."

"Good. They deserve each other."

Phoebe opened her mouth to defend Paravent, then

shut it again. What was it about those two, that they brought out the worst in each other? Tamás turned sullen and Paravent bossy. But Tamás would have to understand, Phoebe *needed* Paravent. Who else was going to fight the Enchanter?

Tamás was checking over the sections of his flute. Then he rolled up his sleeve and polished each piece on the skin of his forearm. "Like a chamois cloth," he explained. "Did you know chamois's made of goatskin? Or it's supposed to be."

"Tamás, how long have you been playing the flute?"

Tamás shrugged. "It was my grandfather's flute. He went to the Royal Music University in Budapest when he was just sixteen years old. But later he got in trouble with the Russians." Tamás stroked his thumb over the wood. "My grandfather—even when he was old he could play four measures of a sustained adagio in one breath, on this wood flute. That Professor Bacall at the college, he wants me to switch to metal. 'Because it's easier to play,' he says. My grandfather would've told him, 'You want easy, whistle through your teeth.'"

"But is he still alive, your grandfather? Did he make recordings?"

Tamás shook his head. "No. He died. And the Russians never let him perform anywhere, or travel. He worked in the sausage factory with my father."

Then he was silent awhile, staring up into the branches of the trees that crowded beside the trail as if they were hung with pictures from that other time, or with music.

Phoebe broke the silence, at last, saying, "But you must have a teacher here, too. It can't be—not Mrs. Gorton?"

At first Tamás didn't answer, just turned his face to her with the old empty-windowed look. Then he startled Phoebe by snarling suddenly, "She treats me like a trick dog. 'Sit up and beg, *dear*!'" He tried to twist the long line of his mouth into a fussy bow, like Mrs. Gorton's.

"But—"

"My mother cleans house for Professor Bacall, from the college. Sometimes I go to him."

"But, Tamás, don't you even want to be in Orchestra?"

He shrugged again, hunching up one shoulder so she couldn't see his face.

"God, Tamás, you could win scholarships. I bet you didn't even try out for Junior Philharmonic. You didn't, did you?"

Tamás mumbled something about his grades.

"Yeah, really—like you couldn't get good grades if you wanted! I heard you name all those armor parts. You just fake that dumb act."

Tamás was busy stowing the parts of his flute. When he finished he rocked to his feet and set off down the path alone. But he only went a few paces, then stopped with his back to Phoebe.

She shouted after him, "For God's sake, Tamás! How

can you expect people to like you if you won't show them anything to like?"

He started walking again. Phoebe trailed after him, talking at his back. "I bet if they had a contest for who could screw up his life in the most dumb-ass way possible, you'd win second prize. You'd come in right after the guy who drinks a bunch of beer and drives ninety miles an hour into a telephone pole."

Tamás walked faster. The springy gait of his goat feet didn't match the hunch of his shoulders.

"Listen, Tamás, I'm not trying to be mean. But you have to let people see who you are. Even Mrs. Gorton, how can she—"

Tamás swung around, his eyes angry, his mouth open to say something angry. But meeting Phoebe face-to-face, so close to him, he froze. The words seemed to get stuck in his throat.

Phoebe felt sorry she'd been so rough on him, after he'd practically risked his life to save her from the boy with the fork. She held out her hand to Tamás. "Look, let's shake and be friends," she said.

Tamás blushed red, then purple. His hand made little sawing motions in the air as he failed to extend it all the way or bring it back down to his side.

Phoebe took it and shook it briefly.

They walked on down the trail, neither one speaking, each careful not to look at the other. This time it was Tamás who broke the silence.

"Phoebe," he said, "when you were on the bridge, you told me—I mean, you said you were standing on the bridge and it was like the Enchanter's glass tried to get you, right?"

Phoebe nodded. She sneaked a glance at Tamás. He was frowning, but not, she thought, at her.

"Tell me, what were you thinking about, just at that moment?"

"I don't know," said Phoebe. "I was just kind of looking at the water, you know. It was Friday, about two or three in the afternoon, and—"

"What were you doing not in school?"

"I was skipping. I told you that before. And I was thinking... I was kind of pretending the bridge was a boat, you know, and I was going away someplace—"

"That's it!" Tamás's face looked shiny with excitement. "Skipping, hiding, and pretending—that's just what I was doing, too. No, wait—" He waved a hand to keep Phoebe from interrupting. "Listen. It was the day Mrs. Gorton was coming to see my mother. She has this idea, see, that I'm *trainable*." His face darkened and for a moment he looked quite ferocious. "She kept trying to get my mother to go talk to her at school—but my mother wouldn't, of course. So in the end Mrs. Gorton made an appointment to come to our house. She wants me to be in that Junior Philharmonic."

"Tamás, that's great!"

"*No*. She thinks I'm like those people you see on

TV—like, they're idiots but they can recite the Manhattan telephone book or something. A trick animal."

"But you could *show* her—"

"No. Listen, I was telling you ... I hid. I went down in the woods and leaned against a tree until it got dark. Because I figured she'd never get my mother to understand anything if I wasn't there to translate. And ... and I pretended. I pretended Professor Bacall wrote to the Juilliard School for me, and sent them tapes. Of me, playing the flute. Then they—they wanted—" Tamás's face was on fire. He drew a strangled-sounding breath and went on, "Anyway. That's when it happened. I got caught, see what I mean?"

"No, I *don't* see. All I see is you just blew off your best chance ever to—"

"Phoebe, think about the subject. I was hiding. I was pretending."

"Oh!"

"So that's when he gets you, see? That's when the Enchanter gets power over you."

"Yes ... But what about the others? Some of them are grown-ups. They don't skip or pretend. Like Merlin, for instance—"

"Well, so what about Merlin?" said Tamás impatiently.

Phoebe burst into tears.

It took forever to squeeze the story out, in the spaces between gulps and sniffles. How she'd seen the little wizard in the paperweight and thought... And Pop didn't seem to *care* about anything anymore, or listen when she... Then afterwards she couldn't even see him when she looked at him through the glass.

Tamás was ready to sacrifice the waxed paper for a handkerchief. Phoebe said it wouldn't work anyway. She used her sleeve.

"... so he went on sabbatical for half a year," she said, pushing the damp ends of her hair behind her ears. "That's what it's called when college professors take time off, like to write a book or something. And he was actually working on this book. He's been working on it for years. He said it was the best thing he'd ever started, only..." She pushed her hair back again with trembling fingers. Tamás took her hand and patted it.

"Only, he didn't do anything. On the book, I mean. The doctor told him he was well enough to work if he wanted. But it was like it was so important to him it kind of scared him, you know? Then in September he didn't go back to teaching. He just kind of drifted into retirement. I see what you mean about skipping. It fits, doesn't it?"

They had walked on for some time under the lengthening shadows of the forest when Tamás suddenly exclaimed, "Why? *Why* does he do this—the Enchanter?"

"Well," said Phoebe, "he's a collector, right? People who collect stuff can get really crazy about it. Like, look at what they pay for art—millions of dollars, sometimes, just for one piece."

"But that's *art*."

"So, think about it. Paravent said what you see in the paperweight is the perfect image of the mind. Isn't that what art is supposed to be?"

Tamás still looked doubtful. "What the Enchanter does—that's evil, Phoebe. There's nothing *evil* about collecting art."

"There is if you're stealing it," said Phoebe.

About sunset they came around a long curve of the trail and saw a ruined cottage. The way was very broad here, and set about with huge knotted oak trees. The river was just visible some distance away, in glimpses down a wooded slope.

Near the water was a village. They almost didn't see it, in the failing light, so cleverly was every cottage nestled in some fold of the ground or beside one of the great old oaks. Also, the house roofs were weather-stained thatch or mossy wooden shingles, hard to distinguish from the colors of the surrounding forest. But beyond a thicket of evergreens rose the towers of what seemed to be a castle.

"Do you think it's the Enchanter's?" asked Tamás, looking pale and wide eyed in the dusk.

"No," said Phoebe, shortly. She was examining the cottage closest to the trail. Its roof was caved in and the walls collapsed, a total ruin.

"I don't see any lights. No smoke," said Tamás, looking out over the village. "No dogs, or anything. Do you think there's anybody here?"

"No," said Phoebe.

Tamás came to stand beside her and stare at the wrecked cottage. "I wonder what happened here. It looks like somebody just stomped on it."

"Yes," said Phoebe in a queer voice, "they did."

"Not more giants!"

"No, it—it wouldn't have to be anybody big. I think the cottage . . . used to be smaller."

Because this must be Old Angelo's stepped-on cottage, thought Phoebe, *and the rest of the Civilization on the riverbank.* Somehow, in the Life of the Mind, they had grown to full size.

"Look," she said, "you see where the big boulder is, right next to that clump of bushes? Around the other side of that I think we'll find another cottage. It's getting dark; we could spend the night there. Nobody would care."

"I don't understand," said Tamás. "How do you—"

"I'll tell you," said Phoebe.

It took a lot of telling, about allegory and the Life of the Mind. She wanted to show him how everything fit in, the Black Knight and the IN pavilion . . . She skipped lightly over the geeks, in case Tamás might feel sensitive. But he listened without interrupting, except to make, once or twice, little startled noises. Until she reached the part about the Civilization—

"It was important to me, you see," said Phoebe. "It looks big now because it was a big deal in my mind."

Then Tamás said, "The doll you lost—the little one in a blue dress—that one was your favorite?"

"Angelina, yes. But about what Staci said, about the Life—"

"Wait. A blue dress of shiny material, right? And there was another, too, in plain brown."

"How did you know that?"

"I'm sorry," said Tamás, "I think I know who stepped on the house and took your dolls, Angelina and... who was the other?"

"Giles. I guess." Giles the Night Watchman was the only other one she'd missed. But why worry about that now, when they had important stuff to discuss?

"It was Eva," said Tamás. "My little sister, you know, Eva? She showed them to me. She made them a farm in our garden. Actually I think it was a snail ranch. But I will tell her she has to give them back to you."

So Angelina had ditched the gluey Prince and eloped with Giles the Watchman! Phoebe looked in wonder over the dark harbor and the odd, twisted turrets of the castle behind its screen of trees. A slim moon glimmered like an ensign above the topmost turret. "Never mind," she told Tamás. "You tell Eva she can keep them if she wants."

CHAPTER X

TAMÁS HORVATH

In such a salvage wight, of brutish kynd,
Amongst wilde beastes in desert forrests bred,
It is most straunge and wonderfull to fynd
So milde humanity, and perfect gentle mynd.

Let me therefore this favour for him finde,
That ye will not your wrath upon him wreake...
—*The Faerie Queene*, VI, 5

PHOEBE TOLD TAMÁS the place where they were planning to spend the night belonged to the Widow Moss and her daughter, Fern. Fern used to keep a pet pill bug, but it ran away. They found the cottage right where Phoebe said it would be, around back of the boulder. But her heart sank at the first sight of it in the failing light, a hovel of crumbling sod bricks and moss-grown thatch. The door sagged open on one hinge. There weren't any windows.

Tamás called, "Hello? Anybody here?" He ducked his head to peer in at the low doorway. "Looks deserted."

"Do you think there's spiders in there, in the dark?" Phoebe spoke in a whisper, for no reason she could explain.

Tamás said, "If we kick that door open all the way we'll get some light for maybe half an hour. Do you want me to go in first?"

Inside was dry, except for a mud puddle near the door, and apparently spiderless. A coarse woven rug covered part of the dirt floor. In the middle of the single room stood a split-log table with two rocks for seats. There was a clutter of wooden implements on the table, and a heap of bedding against the far wall.

That was all. Phoebe let out a breath she hadn't realized she'd been holding.

The People were really gone. Now that she was sure, she could admit to herself she'd been very uneasy about meeting people she'd made herself out of curler pins and glue. Those round, blank pink faces! Phoebe shuddered. Though she had loved the Civilization once . . . Maybe she still did, the way she still loved Hubert the Bear, who sat all day propped against the pillow of her bed at home. But she'd known the game was finished when she'd lost Angelina. The life had gone out of it.

Tamás called her over to the table. "Phoebe, look! Here's food." He held up a round brown loaf. A wooden bowl contained a dollop of dark jam speckled with seeds.

"I feel like Goldilocks," said Phoebe. But she ate when Tamás tore the bread into chunks and slathered them with jam. The bread was dense and moist and slightly bitter.

"I'll bet you anything this is made with acorns," she said, chewing.

The feeling of strangeness that had troubled her spirits since she'd recognized Old Angelo's ruined cottage was passing away. This food, so homey and real, belonged to her. I *made all this*, she thought, smoothing her hand over the tabletop. *Someday I'll bring Eva down here and show her how to make the People.*

Tamás went and stood in the doorway to play his flute, though by now the day was gone. His body swayed and jerked, or curved tenderly over the emerging melody.

Once he asked her, "Do you think it sounded shallow in the second register?"

"Not to me," said Phoebe. But she was too shy to tell him how it did sound, clear as the young moonlight spilling in at the doorway. Instead she said, "You know what? I've heard you play a bunch of times. Only, I never knew it was you. There's this place down by the river near your house. I used to go there and pretend like it was an enchanted glade. And the music was the magic."

"Music *is* magic," said Tamás.

The bedding turned out to be only a stack of mats woven from the same coarse moss gray fiber as the rug. Under these was a big heap of dried leaves and ferns.

Phoebe and Tamás made up two smaller heaps and spread them with mats, then piled the rest up over themselves. It was fun, messing with the leaf piles, and the resulting nests were warm and sweet smelling, though scratchy.

Phoebe couldn't sleep. She started thinking about home. Althea must be crazy with worry by now, unless... unless some zombie had gone home in Phoebe's place. But surely her own mother would notice the difference!

Then she remembered Althea in the kitchen, asking about the tryouts. Phoebe had made a big deal of scraping her plate so she wouldn't have to answer. She wondered how long it had been since she'd talked to her mother like a human being, not all the time lying and ducking.

"Are you awake?" asked Tamás, softly. "What are you thinking about?"

"Oh, I... I was just thinking about my mother. She'd have a nervous breakdown if she knew I was spending the night with some boy." Then Phoebe had to grit her teeth to keep from howling with embarrassment. How could she have said that, out loud, and to Tamás Horvath of all people?

"Well," said Tamás, "I'm only half a boy after all."

They were quiet for a while. Then Phoebe, forgetting that Tamás might have gone to sleep, said, "Althea's so edgy all the time now! It seems like she's always picking at me. Especially with Pop being... the way he is. And she's all torn up about this tour she's supposed to go on this spring with the Bartók viola concerto. Are you awake?"

"Yes. It's a great piece of music."

"Yeah, it's a big opportunity for her. She knows that, but . . . well, it's pretty late to start your career as a concert soloist when you're fifty-three years old. I think she's got cold feet."

It was surprisingly easy to talk to Tamás in the dark. Phoebe could feel him listening, though he didn't say much. And she didn't have to look at those goat legs. It was just like he was a regular person.

"I think when my mother was a kid she dreamed about being a big concert star," she told him. "Then when she got to be about my age she had this little brother, and it turned out *he* was the really big star. I asked her once if it wasn't just because he was the boy, but she said no, he had a real talent. It was like she was mad that I even asked the question."

"So what happened to this brother?" said Tamás.

"He fell off the top step of a bus and broke his neck. But by that time Althea'd married, and then there was me."

Tamás grunted. "And now you're supposed to get the big talent, huh?"

"I don't know . . ."

"But, Phoebe, don't you even *want* to play? You're the

only one in that stupid orchestra who has any style at all!"

"Sure I want to! It's just . . . I can't want to as much as *Althea* wants." Phoebe squirmed in her bed and scattered half her leaf covering. "I don't ever seem to want *anything* as much as Althea does. Sometimes, it makes me feel like I'm only half-real, you know what I mean?"

"No," said Tamás.

They were quiet while Phoebe collected her leaves. Then she said, "Tell me about your family," so he wouldn't go to sleep. "Does anybody else play music?"

"My father played the violin."

"Was he good?"

"No. He played at weddings—gypsy love-song stuff. In Hungary he was manager of a sausage factory. But he wanted to come here, to America. I can remember him telling us, 'There's opportunity for everybody in America.'"

"Is he dead?" asked Phoebe, gently.

"No! Why do you say that?"

"I'm sorry—I just never saw him, I guess. And you made it sound—"

"He went back," said Tamás.

"Back? You mean back to Hungary? Why?"

"My father said, 'In our country everything is changing. There's work for patriots to do.' Eva was too little. She was just born when we got here." Tamás was whispering, his voice half-lost in the sound of dry leaves rustling. "My father said, 'Be a big boy, learn English, look after the women until I send—'" He cleared his throat. "That was four, five years ago. Right now in Hungary, it's mostly unemployment. Lots of work for patriots, not much for sausage managers. He'll never send."

Phoebe reached for his hand but couldn't find it in the dark. "Your English is great," she said, because she couldn't think of anything else. To her surprise it seemed to cheer him up.

"Do you remember in third grade?" he said. "I was a year older than everybody, and I didn't know anything. No English at all, only 'yes,' 'thank you,' and 'boop-boop'!" He laughed. "Boop-boop! Some cartoon guy said that on TV, and I thought it was real English words."

Phoebe lay rigid with shame, her outstretched arm growing cold. When Tamás spoke again his mood seemed to have shifted. His tone was carefully matter-of-fact.

"In America, my mother is afraid of everything. She's afraid of the voices in the telephone talking English. I think maybe she's a little crazy. Probably you already noticed."

"Tamás, how can you *say* that—she's your *mother*! I mean, maybe she's worried like crazy, and lonely. She must be awfully lonely. That could make anybody act strange. But she couldn't be, like, *crazy*."

"How do I know?"

"Because... then wouldn't you be, too? That's the kind of thing people inherit. And there's nothing wrong with *you*. Or Eva."

"No... There's nothing wrong with our Evike. She's cute, isn't she?"

"And bright. Anybody can tell she's not being brought up by crazy people."

Tamás said, "How come your hand's so cold? You need more leaves?" And later, when he'd built up a crackling pyramid over her, "Do you hate it a lot that I'm a goat?"

"I don't notice it too much anymore."

In the morning it rained, and Tamás had to spend half an hour warming and rubbing his flute. He was terrified that the wood might swell and crack. Then the sun came out and the whole world glittered.

Phoebe was almost ashamed to suggest they put off the quest for one more morning, to explore the village and harbor, but she did.

"Besides," she said, "it's not like we know what to do, once we get to Mr. Barnes's store. Or even if it'll be where we think it is. Maybe it would be better if we wait here, at least until we know if Paravent's coming."

"Something will be there," said Tamás, ignoring her suggestion about Paravent. "We can start by smashing all the glass."

"He's not going to let us just waltz in, you know. He's Archimago the Enchanter."

"He's just one little old guy," said Tamás. "How's he going to stop us?" But he seemed just as happy to explore the Civilization with Phoebe.

That morning was rich in discoveries. Behind the cottage they found a stone trough half-filled with husked acorns. Phoebe led the way to a little round dell where there was an outdoor school with moss-covered benches for the pupils. Under the teacher's platform they found a stack of wooden shingles and sticks of charcoal for writing. By sprinkling fine dust on the shingles and blowing it across, they could make out some of the old writing exercises.

There were other kinds of discoveries as well, about favorite music or books or people they knew at school.

"*Cyrano*," said Phoebe as they were heading across the castle courtyard. "Did you ever see that movie? I cried so much I had to wear a bag of frozen peas over my nose at dinner."

Tamás liked Fred Astaire. Phoebe and Tamás tap-danced all around the cobbled yard. Goat feet worked great for tapping.

The castle turned out to be the only disappointment of the morning. The whole place had an unpleasant, moldy smell, and the turrets had no inside space at all, only wooden stairways that wound round and round the outsides of the odd-shaped spires. The wood looked much too rotten and punky to trust with their weight. Tamás said he didn't like high places, anyway.

Then out back of a waterlogged cottage near the harbor they came upon a canoe propped up on trestles. Someone had been carving all over it in intricate patterns like bark.

Full of wonder, Phoebe traced the pattern of grooves with her fingers. "This really was just bark when I made it," she told Tamás.

"It's amazing that you made all this," he said. "I wish I could've done some, too."

"Well, I didn't exactly make it like this. This is more like I *imagined* it."

"That's the start, isn't it?" said Tamás. "First you imagine, then you make. Like writing music."

They began climbing back up the hill to the trail. Their pockets bulged with hunks of acorn bread gleaned from the cottages.

"The thing is," said Phoebe, "sometimes you just imagine stuff so you don't have to do anything. So you can pretend it doesn't matter."

"Yes . . ."

Then Tamás stopped talking, and she thought he'd dropped the subject. When he spoke again she was fingering the lumps in her arming doublet to find her piece of glass.

"I think we must have two imaginations," he said, "one for making things, and one just for fooling ourselves. Or like your glass," he added as she drew it out of her doublet, "one imagination, but with two different sides to look through."

Phoebe stopped short as if she'd walked into a glass wall.

"God, Tamás, I can't believe you're so smart!"

"What did I do now?"

"Do? You just solved the mystery, that's what you did. See, the glass made all this happen—showed us the Life of the Mind, I mean—because it works like the imagination. It's like I told you, the dark glass that Spenser said you're supposed to look through to see what things really mean."

She held out the glass to Tamás, but he seemed not to want to touch it.

"I thought you weren't supposed to look through it," he said. "Isn't that what Paravent told you? Because if you do the Enchanter can get you. That's what he said."

"Yes, but that's the whole point, don't you see? *It's got two sides*. Like you said about imagination: one side for when you're being creative, and the other for when you're fooling yourself. And we already figured out it's when you're fooling yourself that the Enchanter gets power over you, right?"

Then Tamás took the glass and held it up to the light. The round, polished side reflected the sheen of the sky. He turned it over in his hand. The light seemed to fall into the broken side and stay, not reflecting back, so that the glass looked darker. But it made a bright, prism-tinted spot on his palm.

"So which side is which, do you think?" he said.

Phoebe gnawed her lip. "Well, sometimes if you look through the broken side stuff comes out all mixed up and strange. I mean, it seems every time I look through it I see something bad."

"Maybe that's just what the poet guy meant by calling it the *dark* glass."

She shook her head. Hadn't Paravent told her it was okay to use the shiny side, that time when she'd put on the armor and wanted to see how she looked? It was only because the glass was buckled in under her armor that she'd used that stupid pink mirror and fooled herself into believing she was a real knight.

"Oh, rats!" she cried. "I wish Pop was here. He could explain everything, I bet. Like about allegory. That's what he used to teach about at the college."

"So what about this allegory stuff," said Tamás. "Does it have rules so you can tell what means what?"

"Sort of... At least there're some things that always mean pretty much the same. Like, uh, well—like lambs, for instance. When there's a lamb in an allegory poem you're not supposed to think, like, Lambs are stupid. Or, Lamb chops for dinner. You're supposed to think, Lambs are innocent. That's the rule."

"But not goats, huh?"

"I don't think so." Thinking about it, she decided goats in Spenser meant something like the animal side of human nature. Actually, like ... sex.

"Or take horses," Phoebe said quickly. "The horse and his rider were supposed to be the mind and the feelings. So in allegory stories there's almost always some guy who can't control his horse, because he's too angry or sexy or something and he—uh—I mean—" Too late, Phoebe realized where her example was leading. She was the only one who hadn't been able to control her horse.

"Well," said Tamás, "it was Sir Paravent who showed up with that stupid horse in the first place. Even if it's not allegory it's got to mean *something* that he got hold of the only warhorse since the dawn of time that's afraid of armor."

"But he didn't know that!"

"Why not? We both noticed it right away."

"*You* noticed it," said Phoebe, crossly.

They'd come to the trail, and now Phoebe began to hurry, taking long steps so that Tamás almost had to skip to keep pace with her. But she said, "I wish we'd waited for Sir Paravent. I'd feel a whole lot safer if he was with us."

Tamás took hold of her sleeve to make her stop. "Listen, Phoebe, it's your glass," he said, "not mine or Paravent's. Why don't you just hold it up and look at something—look at me, if you want—through both sides, one after the other? Then you can decide which one looks more like the truth."

He tried to hand the glass back to her, but she wouldn't take it.

"I don't know ... Anyway, it wouldn't work. The glass doesn't work that way, because you *can't* look through the polished side. It only reflects." She tried to shrug off his hand, but he held on. "Let's just wait before we try any experiments, okay?"

"Wait for what?"

"For Paravent, of course. He's bound to catch up with us sooner or later, if we stick to the trail. Especially after we wasted all morning—"

Tamás made an odd sound, "*houh,*" like someone bursting a blown-up paper bag. He stuffed the glass through a gash in the side of her arming doublet, jamming it in so hard he hurt her and spun her partway around. Phoebe yelped, mainly from surprise. Then she froze, open mouthed.

Paravent stood on the path. He'd left the horses behind and was wearing black jeans, like at Staci's pavilion, plus a tough-looking leather jacket. The jacket was unzipped to let the sunlight glint off the mirror-polished breastplate underneath. A long sword swung from his hip.

He raised his hand in a salute. The gesture seemed oddly tentative, unless he was just pushing back his hair.

"Phoebe!" he called. "Thank heaven I've found you at last!"

Phoebe sketched a wave. She couldn't think of anything to say. As Paravent walked toward her she noticed that his eyes looked puffy, as if he'd lost sleep. She felt a pang of guilt. It had never occurred to her that he might really *worry*.

Then his gaze hardened as it shifted to Tamás, standing beside her with his hand still on her sleeve. Paravent's hand drifted to the pommel of his sword.

"Phoebe, why did you run away?" he said. "I have been nearly mazed with dread."

Tamás made a noise like a goat and it made Phoebe mad. As soon as anybody came he had to start acting idiotic all over again. She jerked away from Tamás—but then Sir Paravent seemed to misunderstand her action, because he leapt forward, sweeping her up in one arm but keeping his sword arm free. The silver blade flashed as he drew and swung it aloft.

Phoebe shrieked. She clutched at Paravent's sword arm, dragging it down. She could hear the blade slicing the air as it descended. Then somehow the sword got mixed up with her feet. She stumbled, but she had the sense to fall against Paravent, so he lost his balance as well. They went down together in a heap, with Tamás dancing around them and hollering.

"You cut her! You *murderer*!"

Tamás would have helped her up, but she slapped his hands away.

"Phoebe, you're *bleeding*."

"No, I'm not." But her ear was stinging, and when she reached up to touch it her hand came away smeared with blood. "It's only a scratch. For heaven's sake, Tamás, I only scraped it on the zipper of his jacket when we fell."

Sir Paravent roused himself and produced a powder blue handkerchief to dab at the blood. Phoebe had to admit she felt a little shaky, though the cut wasn't serious; so Paravent put his arm around her.

His blue eyes under the sleepy-looking lids searched her face. "Look, I'm sorry about the goat; I didn't mean to scare the poor kid. I was just so worried about you—I took him for some wild thing out of the woods."

And, really, Tamás did look wild. He'd walked a little way apart from Phoebe and Paravent and stood gritting his jaw, as if he meant to bite somebody. After three nights of sleeping rough, his thick dark hair looked like he'd blow-dried it in a hurricane.

Phoebe's hand stole up to her own hair. "Tamás is okay," she said. "He's just . . . kind of unusual."

"He's jealous, poor little beast," said Paravent, smiling into her eyes. He smoothed the hair away from her face, and the tips of his fingers lingered, just for a moment, on her cheek.

CHAPTER XI

LEWIS BARNES

For by his mightie science he could take
As many formes and shapes in seeming wise,
As ever Proteus to himselfe could make:
Sometime a fowle, sometime a fish in lake,
Now like a foxe, now like a dragon fell,
That of himselfe he oft for feare would quake,
And oft would flie away.

—*The Faerie Queene*, I, 2

THE THREE AGREED TO FOLLOW the trail until they came to the Steephill Road bridge. There they would stop to make plans before approaching Archimago's lair. Or rather, Phoebe and Paravent agreed, while Tamás glowered and dug grooves in the trail with the point of his hoof.

They set out in silence, walking in a line with Paravent leading—though the path was wide enough, most places, for two or three to walk together. Clouds gathered in the sky and thickened, but the afternoon was unseasonably warm. Phoebe began to feel sticky in her padded clothes. Her hair itched, and her leg muscles ached. Tamás bickered at Paravent, who ignored him and then made cracks about him to Phoebe. Phoebe decided she was sick of them both.

She lagged behind in a place where a tall beech tree grew right in the middle of the path. She leaned her cheek against the cool gray bark, fingering a neatly pleated new leaf just scrolling out of its coppery sheath. The air here smelled spicy with beech mast and a whiff of skunk cabbage.

"I know where we are," she said aloud.

Tamás and Paravent on the path ahead stopped to look back at her.

"This beech tree," she said, "this is where you have to get off the path to find my enchanted glade. You can smell the swamp. And just around that curve ahead is where the gravel starts, for the swimming hole. You know, where the bridge is."

"Then it's time to make plans," said Tamás.

But Paravent said, "Tell me about this enchanted glade. I know not of it."

Phoebe told him it was only a game. She'd always had the feeling it was a special place, and once when she was just a kid she'd buried a magic ring there.

"A magic ring?" Paravent's eyebrows climbed.

"Oh, it wasn't magic *really*. It was just a cheap brass ring with a music sign on it. I found it here, near the glade, and pretended like it was a wishing ring. Then my mother told me to throw it away, so I brought it back to the enchanted glade and buried it instead. I don't know why I'm rabbitting on about this now. It was just—"

"A brass ring with a treble clef where the stone is supposed to go," said Tamás.

"How did you know?"

"It was mine. I won it for a music prize in school. In my old school, where I used to live—"

Paravent, with his hand half raised to smooth back his hair, suddenly clutched his forehead and groaned aloud. "Fool that I am!"

Tamás quirked up one eyebrow. "So you finally noticed."

Paravent spun away on his heel, then came striding back, a new light of determination in his eye. "We stand on the very doorstep of fell Archimago," he declared, "yet we chatter like little birds, unmindful of the fox. I call myself to blame—I, a knight, the sworn defender of the weak! I have taken no care to spy out the snares that even now he lays in our way."

"What should we do?" Phoebe spoke in a whisper, infected by his alarm.

Tamás answered, "March right up to the door and barge in! What else can we do? Besides, it's hiding and sulking around that gets you in trouble with this guy. We know that."

"A strategem fit for a horned beast!" Paravent screwed up his lips as if the words had a disgusting taste. "Yet subtle Archimago can devise a hundred forms and shapes in seeming truth. Then may you batter your tender horns against a rock, or leap into the river, fleeing phantom fire."

"Just tell me one thing," said Tamás. "Why do you talk like that? You aren't a real knight, any more than I'm a real goat. So what's with this Middle Ages talk? You never even told us—"

"He told *me*," said Phoebe, to make Tamás shut up. "What's the *matter* with you guys? We're supposed to be doing a quest. It's real important to a bunch of people. For all we know, this fighting is some kind of plot by the Enchanter, to mess with our heads so we don't succeed."

Tamás wouldn't meet her eyes. "No, it's not," he mumbled.

But Paravent said, "You speak wisely, as ever."

His idea was for someone to go on alone, to scout for possible attackers or enchanted booby traps. He looked pointedly at Tamás, who didn't volunteer.

"Well," said Phoebe, with the sense of dropping into a hole created by Tamás's silence, "well, since I have the glass, maybe I—"

"Nay, give it to me," said Paravent, reaching out his hand.

But Phoebe wouldn't. "Tamás and I figured it has something to do with the way I see things. So I think I ought to be the one to keep it, don't you?"

Paravent drew in his chin and blinked at her. "Of course. I only meant the duty should be mine, to go ahead." He raised his outstretched hand as if to recite the Boy Scout's pledge. "My vow of knighthood bids me to protect all gentle ladies—and persons of low station."

Tamás shrugged rudely.

Phoebe looked down at her feet. She hated the way Sir Paravent was always taking digs at Tamás. Besides, she couldn't help wondering why Paravent kept wanting her to give him the glass... Like at Staci's pavilion, she thought suddenly, when her clothes disappeared—had Paravent stolen them, to search her pockets? But that was crazy. Paravent was a knight armed with a sword. If he wanted anything of hers, why not just take it?

Then she realized he was still waiting for her to speak. She reddened and said, "It's okay with me if you want to be the scout. Tamás and I can wait here, by this tree."

Sir Paravent went down on one knee and kissed Phoebe's hands. His lips were warm and full, her fingers small and cold and, she noticed, not very clean.

Paravent is okay, she thought, feeling suddenly anxious for him. If he was bossy sometimes, he was just trying to protect her. He was that knight-in-shining-armor type. Phoebe watched him walk away, head high and sword drawn, until he disappeared around the bend in the path. Then she turned on Tamás.

"That was a nasty crack you made about the way he talks. He probably can't help it, poor guy, any more than you can help looking like a goat."

She expected Tamás to get mad. Maybe she wanted him to, so they could have a good argument and clear the air. But Tamás only rubbed his hands down over his face, as if he was too tired to fight.

"I think I went around for years *acting* like a goat, when I could've helped it if I tried," he said. "Who is Paravent, really? Did he tell you?"

"I, uh, I think he did, that night at Staci's, but I... That is, a lot of stuff was going on and I kind of forgot."

Tamás picked at the wool of his goat legs. "You really like him, huh?"

"Not all that much... But, like, he tries so hard. I don't want him to feel bad."

Tamás nodded thoughtfully. Then his ears twitched forward and he tugged at them, exasperated by their goatishness. "I hear something," he muttered. "Somebody... It's Paravent, running."

"He can't be coming back *already*," said Phoebe. But then she heard, too.

Sir Paravent appeared, running and stumbling as he ran around the bend in the trail. When Phoebe called out to him he crumpled to his knees and hid his face.

She went and touched his shoulder. "Paravent, what happened? Are you hurt?"

He raised his face to hers. His hair was wild, and his eyes had too much white around them. "Dragon," he gasped. "A dragon on the bridge." Then he cried, "Oh, Phoebe, forgive me! I am no Saint George."

Phoebe stroked his head. His hair felt as soft and fine as mouse fur. She was terrified that he might weep. But he only stared at her, dry eyed.

"Now what are we going to do?" said Tamás.

"Couldn't we go around some other way?"

"*What* other way?"

"I don't know."

They were silent while Paravent slowly got to his feet, leaning on his sword like an old man with a stick. He smoothed his hair back in place. "I wish—" he said, but didn't say what it was he wished.

"Well, I wish, too," said Tamás bitterly. "I wish this whole stupid business had never happened. I wish all the glass balls would pop like soap bubbles."

"I wish you would shut up," said Phoebe.

Then Paravent, speaking like a man in a dream, said, "We have the enchanted glass, but not the wishing ring."

Tamás snorted. "What are you talking about? There isn't any wishing ring."

"Ah, but there is. Phoebe has told us she buried it near this very spot."

"And *I* told you that ring was just some dopey thing I got in school!"

"To your eyes, perhaps," answered Paravent, "but the maiden is wiser. She knows that desire is the essence of magic. When you wish—"

"Upon a star? In your dreams, mister!"

"In our dreams we all make magic."

"In our dreams we don't make anything," said Tamás, "especially not if you mean daydreams. That's not magic, that's just fooling yourself."

Paravent appealed to Phoebe. "How can you, whose every thought shapes worlds of wonder, doubt the reality of magic?"

Phoebe glanced at Tamás. Why did he glare at her like that, what did he want from her? What did either of them want? She wished like anything she could just go away and be by herself someplace. She turned away and took a step or two off the trail, under the silvery shade of the beech trees.

"Be careful!" shouted Tamás. "You know the ground gets swampy around here somewhere."

Now Paravent left the trail, also, and went striding ahead through the trees. "Do you think you can find the place where you buried the ring?" he called back over his shoulder.

"Not this way!" Phoebe had to hurry to catch up with him. "You're heading the wrong way. Look over there to the left. Can you see how the ground looks kind of brighter? That's where the bluebells grow. I mean, the whitebells. That's the enchanted glade."

"Show me." Paravent took her hand and they moved off together, treading cautiously in case the ground turned boggy. A moment later she caught the first scent of the flowers, heady and rich, laced with excitement.

"That is the scent of magic," said Sir Paravent.

In the Life of the Mind the enchanted glade stretched on farther than the eye could tell, into the deep woods. Overhead, silver branches laced across a dull sky. Under the trees nothing grew except the whitebells, but they grew thick and straight and even as a field of wheat. The trees seemed to cast no shadows on the plain of white. If time moved at all in the enchanted glade, it left no mark of its passing.

"Magic," breathed Phoebe, standing where the first wave of whitebells washed her knees. Sir Paravent, a few steps deeper in, turned to smile back at her. His face looked pale and oddly lit, as if he were shining a flashlight under his chin. All the brightness came from the flowers, so that he seemed to stand in a world turned upside down, the sky at the bottom.

Tamás must have got tired of waiting alone on the path, because Phoebe could hear him calling through the trees. His voice sounded far away and muffled. Then suddenly he came crashing into the glade. One of his legs was caked with black mud.

"Stepped in a hole," he muttered. He seemed dazed at the sight of all those flowers.

Phoebe walked forward with her hands open loosely at her sides, to feel the cool bells brush across her palms. Behind her the bent stems left a wake of silvery green. The scent of bruised flowers hung heavy in the air.

This was the stillest place. No breeze carried the sound of the river. No birds called in the trees. No insects scurried among the flower stems. After a while the silence began to ring in Phoebe's ears, like bells.

"How long have we been walking?" said Tamás, rubbing his eyes. He looked half-asleep.

Phoebe shook her head.

"An hour? Hour and a half? More than that?"

"I don't know! What difference does it make?"

"Because," said Tamás, "we could get lost in here. There's no sense of direction. We could be walking around and around in circles."

"Not so," said Paravent. "The trail of bent stems shows where we have trod before."

Tamás unwrapped the head joint of his flute and played on it like a whistle as he walked.

"Do you have to do that?" Phoebe complained.

"I'm practicing double-tonguing."

"Well, don't. It makes my head ring."

Tamás stuck the head joint back in his pocket. He crumpled the waxed paper and batted it in the air like a Ping-Pong ball until he lost it in a drift of flowers.

Paravent plucked a stem of whitebells. Taking Phoebe's hand, he laid it across her open palm, then stroked her fingers closed around it. He picked stem after stem until she was carrying a great, heady-scented sheaf of flowers. They were not heavy... Perhaps it was the scent, so very sweet, that slowed her steps.

"I'm hungry," said Tamás. "Let's stop and eat some bread." He had to say it more than once before Phoebe heard him. Her head was nodding over her load of flowers. He grabbed her arm and shook it, so the flowers rained around her feet.

"Wake up!" he said. "Your shoes are wet."

Phoebe wished he wouldn't talk so loud; it bothered her ears. Though what he said was true—her shoes were soaked with muddy water. She didn't remember walking through any boggy spots.

"We mustn't stop here," urged Paravent. "We must go on and find the ring."

"Oh... the ring," said Phoebe. She was watching a single bent green stem slowly straighten. Then the stem next to it unbent, and the next. If she stayed still long enough, she thought, the whole green trail that stretched behind her through the glade would turn white again. How beautiful that would be.

"It's impossible to dig for something in a swamp," said Tamás. "Do you even have any idea where we are?"

Phoebe didn't bother to answer. She had stopped worrying about how to find the buried ring. Something would come to her, she supposed. Some plan, or some ... other thing.

Sir Paravent took her hand and led her gently on. Tamás slogged after them, grumbling.

Paravent said gently, "You've dropped your flowers."

"It doesn't matter."

But he was already filling her hands again with fragrant bells.

On and on. Paravent's hand was on her shoulder, guiding her. Phoebe longed to close her eyes. She pillowed her head on her armload of white flowers. How hard it was to walk when her load was so ... heavy and ... Paravent's hand on her shoulder. Heavy ... She felt grateful to him for helping her bend down, sink ... down ... on a bed of flowers.

"Rest now," he murmured, pressing her down among the green stems.

Phoebe turned her cheek to the cool ground. Through the blur of half-closed lashes she could see a gleam of water. Water was soaking into her clothes. It was like when she fell into the water after her fight with Jennifer Gorton, when she'd lain on the river bottom and looked up through stem green water at the shining surface. But then she had felt horribly frightened. Now she was only tired. Phoebe closed her eyes.

A foot splashed down next to Phoebe's ear. Tamás galloped past, treading on her hair.

"Ouch!" she cried, jerking awake. The stillness of the glade was all churned up with angry voices, Tamás and Paravent quarreling.

Phoebe wrapped her arms around her head to blot out the noise, but now she couldn't get comfortable. She was all wet, and the piece of glass in her doublet was digging into her ribs. Then she realized that she was sinking. The ground was soft here, under a sheen of water.

She struggled to sit up. The swamp sucked at her knees, pitching her forward. The hand that she flung out to save herself plunged up to the elbow in icy mud.

"Help," gasped Phoebe. Then, on a rising note of panic, "Paravent, help! *Where are you?*"

"Stay where you are!" It was Tamás's voice, a sharp command.

"No—Tamás, I can't—" She longed to raise her head to look for him, to reach her arms out for somebody to help her. Her hands were black with slime and stank of rotting flowers.

Tamás wasn't talking to her. He was hollering at Paravent. Bewildered, Phoebe let herself slip down on her stomach, spreading her arms to hug the quaking surface of the bog. She tried to straighten her legs. God, how heavy they were, plastered to the mud. Water crawled up around her waist.

"I'm not afraid of you!" yelled Tamás, but his boy's voice cracked and betrayed his lie.

Phoebe threshed her arms back and forth over the shuddering mud. She seized handfuls of green stems to haul herself forward. The mud sighed beneath her as she began to move.

Paravent laughed. In Phoebe's confused mind the sound combined unpleasantly with the sight of white flowers quivering above her head. Paravent . . . *Paravent* had pushed her down in the bog, when she was half-asleep.

Her toes bit into firmer ground. She began to crawl. Then she could push herself up on hands and knees without sinking. But her stomach went on quaking by itself.

Paravent unsheathed his sword—Phoebe knew by the snakelike rattle of the steel, even before she wiped away the wet hair pasted to her face and saw.

Sir Paravent held the sword naked and upright in his hand. He was not looking at her. There was no special expression on his face, but a flush of pink outlined his cheek and jaw. Surrounded by white flowers, he looked like a picture of some noble crusader. A knight in shining armor.

There had been a knight like that in one of the paperweights. But now, thinking back, Phoebe didn't remember breaking that particular paperweight. In fact—hadn't she put it down on a different table, not the one that got knocked over? So where had Paravent come from?

Behind her, Tamás called, "Keep away from him, Phoebe—he's dangerous. He's been leading us in circles all this time. Look at this!"

Paravent started forward, kicking aside the tall stems of the flowers as he strode. Then he began to run. In sudden terror, Phoebe groveled on the ground. But he ran past her, raising the sword to strike at Tamás.

Phoebe screamed out a warning. She rolled over and launched herself, grabbing for Paravent's foot. He staggered slightly, but she couldn't arrest the downward stroke of the sword. He stabbed up a scrap of trash on the ground in front of Tamás.

Phoebe lay flat on her stomach and stared up at the crumpled wad stuck on the point of the sword. Then she looked down at her hands, clasped around Paravent's shoe. It was a white shoe with a gold-tone buckle shaped like a bridle bit.

"Oh, my God," she said, and sat up. She had to find her glass.

"See that, Phoebe?" said Tamás triumphantly, pointing to the trash on the sword. "That's the waxed paper you wrapped around those sandwiches. I used it for my flute, and then I threw it away, hours ago, while he was pretending to lead us—"

Sir Paravent cried, "Shut your mouth!" and thrust his sword at Tamás, who swayed aside but held his ground.

"You forgot to talk like a knight," Tamás said.

Sir Paravent swung again, wildly. "You'd better run, or I'll chop you!"

Phoebe wrestled the glass out of her wet doublet.

Tamás said, "Oh no. I saw you in action once before, remember? The great shining knight beating up on a bunch of little goats. The only time anybody got hurt was when you jerked your horse around and knocked me down. You thought I didn't see what you were doing, huh?"

Then Phoebe held the glass up to her eye and looked through the broken side. The prism glass split the white glade into colors, blue and red and emerald green. In the midst she saw a man ringed in fire with his arm raised to strike. It was Mr. Lewis Barnes, and in his hand was a groundskeeper's stick with a nail at the end.

"Tamás, look! The sword, it's just a stick—" Phoebe's hand wavered; and for an instant she saw Sir Paravent again, and the sword blade flashing down.

Tamás dodged and stumbled to his knees. His hands flew up as if he would plead for mercy.

Phoebe screeched, "It's Mr. Barnes! *Tamás, grab his stick.*"

Sir Paravent aimed a stabbing blow at Tamás's face. But Tamás grabbed the blade.

"Hey!" yelled Paravent.

"Leggo," grunted Tamás.

"I see you, Mr. Barnes," Phoebe sang out, the glass to

her eye once more. "I see that's just a stick; you can't cut Tamás! I see your head is all bald in back. No wonder you keep fussing with your hair! I see—"

Cheeks purple, pale eyes bulging, Mr. Barnes gave up the struggle for his stick. He let go so abruptly that Tamás fell over backward, almost putting his own eye out with the nail.

Mr. Barnes turned on Phoebe.

She snatched the piece of glass out of his reach, behind her back. Instantly it was Sir Paravent who loomed over her. The change happened so fast it rocked her balance and her stomach rose as if she'd stepped into a plunging elevator. Paravent grabbed her by the shoulders. He shook her till her head whipped back and forth. Then she was on the ground and his knee was on her chest, squeezing. Her breath came out in hiccups. He began to pry back her fingers from the glass.

Tamás gave a doglike growl. Paravent took one glance over his shoulder, then scrambled to his feet. He raised his hands in an old man's gesture of dismay.

"Tamás—" Phoebe wheezed for air. "He's got the glass—"

Tamás threw down the sword and stood up. His eyes burned like black holes in space. Phoebe found it easy, now, to believe in Magyar ancestors screaming across the plains of central Asia, leaving scorched destruction in their wake.

Evidently Paravent—or Mr. Barnes—believed this, too. With a muffled grunt he turned and fled, white shoes squelching through the mud.

"After him!" shouted Tamás, grabbing Phoebe's hand to haul her to her feet. "He knows the way out!"

They ran, splashing through water sometimes, stumbling often where the ground was soft. But it was just plain squoosh, not allegorical mire anymore. In an incredibly short time they were free of the glade and running through ordinary woods. But Mr. Barnes, his feet winged with fear of Tamás, ran faster. They lost sight of him, though they could still hear him sometimes, crashing through the underbrush ahead.

Then they were back on the path. Mr. Barnes was nowhere to be seen. Phoebe, sweat blinding her eyes, trod on a stone that rolled under her foot. She fell, crying out in pain.

Tamás helped her to her feet. "Are you all right?" He gripped her by the elbows, in case she couldn't stand alone.

"I think so...My foot...just hurts a...little. I need to...stop." She leaned against him, panting. He rested his chin on the top of her head.

"Tamás... You're tall."

She looked up at his face. Then down at his legs. They were very long legs...human legs, in rumpled brown corduroys. At the ends of the legs were enormous human feet.

Tamás smiled a beautiful smile. "Thank God I have pants," he said.

CHAPTER XII

The Lady Knight

> That brasen dore flew open, and in went Bold Britomart...
> Neither of idle shewes, nor of false charmes aghast.
>
> —*The Faerie Queene*, III, 12

"IT HAPPENED WHILE WE WERE fighting over the sword," said Tamás. "I remember I tripped over something—I went down on my knees—and all of a sudden *I had knees*! But I couldn't stop to think about that then, because Sir Paravent was getting ready to chop my head off."

"Only, Paravent was Mr. Barnes all along, and his sword was just a stick! God, Tamás, you gave him the biggest scare of his life." Carried away with Tamás's triumph, Phoebe forgot for a moment about the lost glass.

"Maybe it looked like a stick to *you*," said Tamás. "*I* thought it was going to slice all my fingers off."

Phoebe couldn't believe he'd grab a sharp-edged sword

just because she told him to. "And how did you change back from a goat? I don't understand *any* of this!"

"I think I understand," said Tamás, slowly. "I changed because I don't . . . I don't see myself like a goat anymore. What I think is, all those people in the paperweights—you don't see them the way they really are. You see them the way they want to see themselves. Like a princess, or a knight in shining armor. It's wishful thinking."

"But, Tamás, you couldn't *wish* to be a goat!"

"Maybe I did. At least, I let other people see me that way. I was always going around acting crazy and dumb so I could say, 'Nobody really sees who I am. They don't hear my music. They can't judge me.' Only you really saw through me."

"Me? I didn't do anything," said Phoebe.

"Yes, you did. I think—" Tamás wrinkled his forehead in concentration, then felt along the wrinkles with his fingers. "No horns!—I think it's because I could trust you, Phoebe. You said, 'Tamás, grab the stick.' So I grabbed, right? It was like you said, 'This is Tamás the person, not just a goat.' So . . . I believed you. I think sometimes you need to trust somebody if you want to change."

Phoebe looked down at his legs. They were actually pretty nice legs. She felt heat creeping up her neck. Then she looked at her own empty hands.

"Oh, Tamás—he took the glass! What are we going to do without it?"

"What were we going to do *with* it?" said Tamás.

"You know! Break into the store. Smash all the glass. Rescue the people!"

"So what do we need the glass for? We can do all those things with our own hands. And feet—" Tamás did a few steps of Fred Astaire. "Come on, Phoebe. We've got him on the run! We've got our own eyes, don't we? And our own imaginations. Mr. Barnes isn't the only one around here who can make stuff up."

"It's not the same thing, Tamás. The glass was *magic*."

Still arguing, they turned up the trail in the direction of the bridge and the swimming hole. The clouds that had dulled the afternoon were passing over and piling up, pink and gold, in the west. On the path the light fell in tiger stripes between long blue shadows of the trees. In another hour it would be dark.

Now they could hear the river again—a muted roar, not the musical gurgle of shallow water over stones.

"That's odd," said Phoebe.

"What is?" said Tamás. But a minute later he stopped and flung out his arm to keep her from walking on.

They'd come to the end of the woods. But there was no gravel beach; or if there was, it was lost at the bottom of a sudden deep ravine that opened up before them like a crooked ax cut.

Phoebe went to peer over the edge. A crumb of earth rolled away from her shoe and fell a thousand feet, disappearing into mist. The river roared invisibly below dark walls of rock. Speechless, she crept back from the edge.

The path followed the line of the precipice. About half a mile away they could see the bridge, like a slender rainbow spanning the ravine. At the far side of the bridge stood a tower. Archimago's lair. From the distance it appeared as a smooth column of black stone, its height doubled by a long finger of dark shadow pointing to the river. The top of the tower broke off in jagged battlements. It was impossible to see any way in.

Phoebe and Tamás didn't talk much. The path was too narrow here to walk side by side. Phoebe went first. Tamás took out his flute and played scraps of songs. A couple of times his breath failed on the attack and messed up his phrasing.

"I just don't like high places," he mumbled.

The bridge was farther away than they'd thought, but even when they got close it looked hardly any wider. They climbed a last stony shoulder of land and stood where the bridge rose from the anchoring rock. It was a single span of stainless steel no more than two feet wide, bent like a bow, and without any rail.

Tamás let out all his breath in a rush. *Whuff!*

Phoebe held up her hand and squinted through her fingers along the polished arch. From where she stood it seemed to curve up into the sunset and vanish there. She rubbed her eyes and saw green bands and negative suns behind her eyelids.

"I don't believe this!" she said fiercely.

"Fine, make it go away," snapped Tamás. Phoebe was ready to snap back, but then she noticed the nervous way he kept rubbing his hands down the back of his pants.

"Come on, Tamás, it can't really be like this! This is Steephill Road, remember? What you see is just because old Archimago Barnes is messing with our heads."

Phoebe spoke more confidently than she felt; but maybe Tamás believed her, because he stopped rubbing his hands and began buttoning his flute into the jean jacket. The top section stuck out awkwardly at his collar. He craned his neck around it.

"Tamás, you were the one who said we should do this, remember? 'March right over and barge in,' you said. We *can't* let him go on fooling us!"

Instead of answering, Tamás took three or four running steps up the steel bridge, then slid back down.

"Slick," he said. "It'll be like trying to walk up the playground slide."

"No, it won't. It's *Steephill Road*. You have to keep saying that to yourself until you believe it. It's the Steephill Road bridge, and it's perfectly flat and dry, and wide enough for a school bus."

"Okay. Yes, I believe you," said Tamás. But he stared down at his feet instead of meeting her eye.

"Come on, I'll go first and tell you what to believe. If we hang around here much longer it'll be dark, and then we'll never make it over."

Tamás nodded yes. "But first I want to spit on my shoes and scuff them in the dirt. That's the best way to get up a slide."

Phoebe started up slowly, setting her feet sideways for better traction. The grit on the bottoms of her shoes made a scratchy, squeaky noise against the metal bridge, like walking on broken glass. She was careful not to look down toward the gaping chasm with the river at the bottom.

Tamás was right behind her. "You're walking on blacktop road," she told him, making it up as they went along from all the hundreds of ordinary times she'd walked across the Steephill bridge. "Here's a mended patch. You can feel the little crumbs of asphalt under your shoes... Now it's tar. See how it kind of ripples in places? That's from getting pushed up in the hot weather. If it was hot you could smell it, too. Here's a screw, stuck in like a fossil. Can't you see it?"

"I can... imagine it, Phoebe."

"You can hold on to my belt if you want." She was still wearing the silken rope she'd taken off the tent flap, knotted around her waist.

"No."

He didn't speak any more, but for a while she could hear him breathing, the air whistling between his teeth fast and shallow. They were nearing the peak of the bridge and the going was harder.

Drops of water beaded the cold steel. Looking up, Phoebe saw she was surrounded by gray mist. It was like they'd climbed right up into the clouds. She had to swallow hard against a sour taste that rose up from her stomach.

"Almost there!" she called to Tamás. "You can see—uh, you can see the store from here. Yeah, there's a light on in the Barn Marché. Cars out front—" Her foot skidded on the wet metal.

"Phoebe—"

"What do you *want*?"

"Phoebe—*I'm going to fall!*"

Her mouth was full of bitter taste. "Hold on—I'm coming to help you."

He was about ten paces behind, crouching on his hands and knees, clutching the narrow span. He hardly seemed to notice as Phoebe edged back along the slide toward him. His head hung down. He kept rocking himself back and forth.

Phoebe sat down in front of him, her legs dangling. "You look like a sick elephant," she said. It was a joke. She hoped he might look up and smile and kind of snap out of it. When he did look up his face was gray, with a sheen of sweat on it.

"Come on, Tamás. We can't go on sitting in the middle of Steephill Road. Any minute now some car's going to come along and run us over."

Only the slightest flicker of his eyelids told her that he heard at all.

"Listen, Tamás, I'm going to tie one end of this rope around your wrist, okay? The other end'll be around me. Then I want you to close your eyes and go just like I tell you, okay?"

His eyes were closed already. He rocked back and forth, back and forth.

"Tamás, *quit that*! You'll make yourself fall!" She reached over and tugged at his flute where it stuck out of the open collar of his jacket.

His eyes popped open and he clutched at the instrument.

She said, "Tamás, listen to me. I need some music. If you don't play some music, I'm just going to lie down in the road and get run over."

He shook his head no, no.

"Yes. You have to help me."

"No... I can't." But his fingers had begun ghosting over the stops.

Now she'd have to figure out how to get up on her feet again. Phoebe began to plan her moves: Reach the left hand behind her and grab the bridge; pivot on her hip; now bring the right leg around... She felt the steel span vibrate under her hands like a tuning fork.

Tamás began to play. He squeaked and fumbled from one note to the next like some kid just learning on a bamboo whistle. Phoebe had got both knees underneath her and was getting ready to push up onto her feet.

But there was something wrong with the bridge. It was shuddering. Phoebe glanced up, toward the peak of the arch. Then she looked down.

It was a deadly mistake.

Below her was the drop. Confusion roared in her ears. The notes of the flute were tiny and miles away. She felt sick and dizzy, and her insides turned to water.

Tamás sang out, "Phoebe, I can see Steephill Road! It's the music—The music makes me see!" With his next breath he sent the flute rippling into the graceful phrases of the Blue Danube waltz.

Phoebe saw nothing but the fog, the ribbon of cold steel clenched between her hands, and the appalling drop beyond. The bridge was shaking and thundering louder than the river. Then she saw eyes, round as moons, scorching through the fog. Tamás grabbed her by the back of her collar and hauled her to her feet.

"Paravent," she sighed, her knees sagging. Paravent had told the truth. He had said there was a dragon on the bridge.

"Yoy, Phoebe, get out of the way! You want to get run over?"

Phoebe covered her face with her hands. She was blinded by the glaring eyes. Nothing but the magic glass could save her now.

"Look out for the car!" shouted Tamás.

He pushed her. She fell in endless slow motion, legs twisting sideways, hands flung up. She heard the dragon scream in triumph. The eyes leapt toward her.

"*Headlights*," she cried.

With a blare of the horn the car swept past.

Phoebe reeled against the bridge railing. All she needed was her own eyes. Her own vision. And when she was too slow to see, she needed somebody like Tamás to give her a shove.

She watched the red taillights retreating all the way up Steephill. The car turned left on River Road. Then she looked down. Under her feet was black tarmac road, and it was dry and flat, and wide enough for a school bus.

The sun had set, leaving only a peach-colored glow on the horizon. The air was clear and smelled of frost. Pale yellow light shone from the front window of the Barn Marché.

Phoebe said, "So, um, which way do you want to go?"

Tamás looked up from polishing a section of his flute. "What do you mean?"

"Well, this is the end, isn't it?" She swept her hand at the road, the swimming hole, all the familiar places. "You could go home now."

"Phoebe, what are you talking about? What about the glass balls—Archimago—your *father*, for God's sake?"

"Oh, I'm going on to the store. I just thought you... I mean, you've done so much already, you don't really have to—you know."

"Are you *crazy*?" Tamás started to wave his arms in the air, then seemed embarrassed by the size of his gesture. He zipped up Phoebe's jacket for her instead. She hadn't noticed until then that she was wearing her own purple jacket and sweatshirt and jeans.

"It's freezing out here, stupid," growled Tamás. "Listen, I'm marching straight in there and smashing every bit of junk in that place. Didn't I tell you that before?"

"Stupid yourself," said Phoebe, feeling suddenly better and warmer all over. "We can't do it like that now, don't you see? This is the real world."

"You're darn right this is the real world! And that means Archimago's on the run. All his tricks are falling apart. Now it's our turn, and we're two against one! What can he do?"

"I don't know about Archimago, but Mr. Barnes can call the police. How do we know he didn't plan it this way, on purpose? We're just kids, Tamás. We can't *fight* him. Not in the real world."

"Want to bet?"

"Tamás, *please*. We could wind up arrested. Then they'd start asking all kinds of questions, like, you know—"

"About my mother," said Tamás grimly, though Phoebe

hadn't been thinking of her. "My mother thinks the FBI is everywhere. They have underground jails where they torture people, like the AVO, the secret police they used to have in Hungary. You can imagine how great she'd do, being questioned by the police. She'd act so nuts they probably really would lock her up."

"We need some kind of plan," said Phoebe.

She wanted to go in alone and talk to Mr. Barnes. "Maybe I'll even cry a little and kind of beg. He'll talk to me, I bet. He knows I don't have the glass, and anyway it was never me he was afraid of. It was you."

Tamás snorted. "He was so sure you'd fall for that fathead Paravent."

"Well, I did feel sorry for him. He was so boring... and I thought he was stuck like that."

"He is. He's a terminal fathead," said Tamás. He didn't like the idea of Phoebe confronting the Enchanter by herself. "What if he pulls some trick? I'm coming with you."

But Phoebe had a different plan. While she was distracting Mr. Barnes in the front room, Tamás would sneak around to the back of the house and climb in by the broken window. His job would be to steal all the paperweights. Once he got safely outside again he could make some noise, like throwing gravel at the side of the building. That would be Phoebe's signal to run for it. They'd rendezvous by the bridge abutment, where she'd hidden her backpack the day she found the magic glass. There they'd smash all the paperweights.

The glass bell tingled as Phoebe pushed open the door of the Barn Marché. Instantly she was overcome with panic, like a bird that's got into a house by mistake and flaps around, crashing into windowpanes, blinded by the electric light. Then her vision cleared, and at the same moment Mr. Barnes looked up from his desk by the front window.

Two bright pink spots appeared on his cheeks like rouge. "What do you want?"

Phoebe squirmed. She mumbled something about having a talk. There were no other customers in the store. Mr. Barnes reached over and flipped the sign in the front window to Closed.

"Where is the boy?" he said.

Phoebe shrugged and spread her hands. Her fingernails were rimmed with black. How many days was it since she'd had a proper wash? Finally she said, "He went home, I guess. It's dinnertime."

"You lost the glass," said Mr. Barnes, as if it had been her own fault.

Phoebe hung her head, but a little pulse of anger throbbed behind her eyes. "You should know," she muttered.

"So now I suppose you want it back, is that it? Is that

what you came here for? Or did you think I'd give you one of my other pieces?"

"Oh, *would* you?"

"Certainly not! What a ridiculous idea." Then he couldn't suppress a little smirk as he folded his white hands on the desk. His own fingernails gleamed.

Phoebe had meant to get down on her knees and make long, begging speeches. She'd planned to cry, if she could manage it. Instead she aimed a short kick at a table loaded with milk-glass knicknacks.

"Who cares about your rotten glass anyway?"

Lewis Barnes rose from his seat. His spectacles flashed. "Beware! I am Archimago the Enchanter!" And for an instant Phoebe really did see the blazing eyes, the flaring aura of the wizard with the flame-colored beard.

She fixed her eyes on the strands of soft white hair combed carefully over his pink scalp. "Big whoop," she said stonily.

Mr. Barnes's hand strayed to his hair. "So, you've had enough of the Life of the Mind, have you?" he said crossly.

"No . . . But, see, it's *my* life. I've figured out it's up to me how I want to look at it."

"Fine words," sniffed Mr. Barnes. "But that dizzy Boyd girl, she could wrap you around her little finger. Now, there's vision for you! Tournaments, everybody battling for the lovely princess—and nothing inside that so-called mind of hers but pink fluff. Boys, cosmetics, whatever vile stuff you kids call music nowadays—"

"Actually, Staci takes ballet, and she's pretty good," Phoebe interrupted. She and Staci hadn't exactly been seeing eye to eye lately, but that didn't make her brainless. "I don't think you really know anything about her mind. You can't just look through people like glass, you know."

"*You* can't. But I am the Arch-Imaginer!"

Phoebe said hotly, "Oh, bull—"

"Temper, temper!" Mr. Barnes shook his finger.

Beyond him, through the archway to the second long room of the store, Phoebe caught a flicker of movement. *Oh, my God*, she thought, *it's the mirror*. She could see Mr. Barnes in the big mirror fixed to the back wall. And—her stomach lurched—she could see the table with the glass paperweights. Mr. Barnes must have moved it so he could keep an eye on them in the mirror. He didn't even need to turn around; if he just raised his eyes to the front window he'd see everything in the mirror reflected back by the window glass. In a few minutes he'd see Tamás stealing the paperweights.

The situation called for drastic measures. Phoebe snatched up a gilded porcelain cup and saucer from a glass-topped stand and held them over her head. "I'll drop this!"

"Put that down!" Mr. Barnes wrung his hands. "That's genuine prewar Nippon Trade Ware!"

"Then give me my glass," said Phoebe.

Mr. Barnes made his eyes into icy slits. "You little hoodlum! Get out of here before I call the police."

"You go right ahead and call them. I'll tell them you

kidnapped me and locked me in the basement. I've been missing for three days, you know."

"You've been missing for one afternoon!" Mr. Barnes sneered. "Oh yes. It's still Saturday in the Real World. You ought to have realized, the shop is never open on Mondays."

His smile was like congealed grease. "The Life of the Mind is so much busier, you know, dear, than ordinary life. I'll tell the police the truth, that you've been playing down by the water with that unsavory Horvath boy. Part of the time I could see you from my window here. For the rest . . . I hate to think what you've been up to! Drugs, I shouldn't wonder, from the way you're carrying on. The authorities ought to have a talk with that boy's family. I understand there's a younger child who might still be saved, if she's placed in foster care."

The Real World seemed to descend on Phoebe like a hard weight. Police. The authorities. How much more terrible they sounded, even, than giants or enchanters!

Mr. Barnes took a step toward her, reaching out for the cup and saucer.

"Stay where you are!" Phoebe rattled the edge of the glass-topped stand. "I'll smash everything on here!"

Mr. Barnes gave an angry hiss, then changed it to a *tsk, tsk!* "Truancy, shoplifting . . . and now vandalism! I don't know why I ever wanted you for my collection, I really don't. You'd only be another silly knight in shining armor. Always trying to rescue someone, isn't that right? Some poor lost cause." He shook his head. "And talk about lost causes! Think how your friends will despise you when they see you chumming up with that lout of a boy."

Phoebe cried, "They will not!" But she remembered the curl of Staci's lip, her grimace—*You don't* like *him, do you?*

"Tamás is incredibly talented," said Phoebe, putting up her chin. "And he's nice. And... and I think he's good looking, too. All he needs is some different clothes."

"That boy's an animal. A congenital idiot! He'll never change."

"He's changed *already*. What do you know about it?"

"I am the Master of Change," said Archimago Barnes.

They glared at each other over the gaudy cups and saucers like two angry cats. Then Phoebe heard a noise. *Clank*.

Her eyes flew to the reflection in the window. While she'd been defending Tamás, she'd forgotten all about what he was supposed to be doing.

Mr. Barnes's eyes followed hers. Then he turned and peered suspiciously into the back room. There was nothing to see, thank God. The little broken window didn't show in the mirror. Tamás must have snapped out a piece of the window glass to enlarge the hole, because he'd been so much smaller when half of him was goat.

Phoebe dumped her cup and saucer on the table and

dodged across the room, colliding with a hostess cart that displayed horribly expensive-looking cut crystal wineglasses. The ringing of the crystal hung on and on in the air.

Mr. Barnes's expression was awful to see. His eyes seemed to grow larger and larger. Phoebe had a crazy notion that his eyeballs would roll right out of their sockets. Only his tiny gold-rimmed spectacles were keeping them in place.

Phoebe picked up two of the toppled glasses and clashed them together. "Give me the paperweight with the wizard!" she demanded.

Mr. Barnes laughed poisonously. "Ah, the little Merlin," he said. "So you guessed about him, did you? But you aren't doing him any favor, you know, *dear*."

He paused to adjust his spectacles, which had slid down his nose. Phoebe thought he was planning how far he'd have to pounce, to get her.

He said, "My little collection are all a pretty sorry lot of misfits, in the Real World. Even if I let one out—*if* I did, I say—he'd come crawling back to me inside of two months."

"That's a lie!"

"I'm telling you this for your own good, young lady! You can get into a lot of hot water, riding to the rescue of someone who won't be saved."

From the back room came sounds of snapping glass

and a muffled *thump*. But Mr. Barnes was intent on Phoebe. She heard the creak of his patent-leather shoes as he began to walk toward her.

"I forget," he said. "How long has the little professor been working on that great scholarly book of his? Five years? Does anyone remember, or care? He was lucky I took him in when I did, before he became the laughing-stock of the English department."

Phoebe shook her head stupidly. She felt as if she were back on the steel bridge, in the fog.

Mr. Barnes shook his head, too. His expression was serious and concerned, like a kind doctor who has to tell bad news. "The truth is, poor Professor Van der Clute is pathetically grateful to be safe inside his glass ball. No more pressure of work, no noisy brat, no nagging wife—"

"I'm not," whispered Phoebe. "Althea doesn't—"

"Yes, there's another loser for you to champion. A cold wife, an undistinguished musician." Mr. Barnes was close enough now to grab her across the glittering display of crystal, but Phoebe didn't move. He went on, "I'd never get your mother into a paperweight, though. No dreaming for her; she sticks to business, doesn't she? A fish tank is what she'd need. Can't you just see her, a nice, neat, cold fish, swimming round and round?"

Phoebe pictured Althea as she'd last seen her, stirring her coffee round and round. What had she been thinking about? She'd been acting so strange, like she'd lost part of herself. The thought struck Phoebe that Althea had been planning to give up her concert tour, to give up her chance at a solo career. She couldn't go away and leave Pop while he still seemed ill. Maybe she couldn't leave Phoebe while she—Had her mother guessed about her problems, about skipping school? Had Althea phoned Mrs. Gorton after all?

Mr. Barnes moved quickly and seized Phoebe's wrists.

She cried wildly, "You don't know anything about people's feelings!" He began to force her hands down, squeezing her wrists to make her release the wineglasses.

"*You* don't have any dreams—you don't have any imagination at all," she hollered at him. "You steal other people's, that's what you do. By yourself you don't understand anything!" She opened her hands to let the glasses crash onto the table.

From the back room came an almighty answering crash. She looked up to see a bright shard slide out of the shattered mirror. Tamás was there. He wasn't stealing the paperweights. He was smashing them against the mirror glass.

Mr. Barnes gave a great scream of rage. Lightning played about his head. He was truly Archimago now. Electric shock zinged up Phoebe's arms from her imprisoned wrists. She brought her foot up under the hostess cart.

Wineglasses leapt up into the air, fell, and spattered up again in sparkling fragments.

Archimago staggered back, his lips writhing with unutterable fury. The air around him seemed to shiver with fragments of glass. Then from the back room came a silvery peal of laughter. Staci Boyd's voice rang out, "Let *me* break the next one!" Phoebe saw a glimmer of pink in the broken mirror as Staci ran to the little table. *She must still be wearing her princess dress.*

The Enchanter flung up his arms and vanished, sucked up into a sudden *whoosh* of smoke. The smoke twisted like a cyclone and resolved into a shape rearing up, dark wings stretching from edge to edge of Phoebe's vision, tail coiling in snakelike loops. A dragon. Its curving talons raked the air, jaws gaping wide with triple tiers of glass-splinter teeth.

Phoebe backed away, snatching up objects of glass to smash or throw. Flames burst from the dragon's maw. Down the whole length of the room, chandeliers twinkled with points of flame. The air crackled. The toppled cart began to burn.

Somebody shouted, "Fire!" From the other room came a babble of voices, crying, laughing. Tamás was calling Phoebe's name. Small fires were starting all around her now. The store lights sizzled and went out. Through a haze of smoke Phoebe could see the dragon's cold green eye shining.

"You think you're so smart," she croaked, her voice harsh with smoke. "You tried to scare me, but you're burning down your own store."

The green eye blinked, then went out.

"Fire... Help!" quavered the voice of Lewis Barnes, in the dark.

Phoebe got down on her hands and knees, below the pall of smoke, and started to crawl toward the door.

She opened her eyes to a dizzy swing of stars.

"Will she be all right?" It was Tamás's voice from somewhere down by her feet. Actually he seemed to be carrying her feet.

"She just got a lungful of smoke. She'll come around," said the person who was carrying her shoulders. He clanked when he walked. He was wearing shining armor.

"Oh, *man*," he said, "I always dreamed I'd rescue some beautiful girl from a burning building!"

"You are only rescuing half of her," said Tamás.

They laid her down on the grass. She stirred and looked around for Tamás.

"It's okay," he said, appearing beside her. "Everybody got out okay."

They heard sirens.

Tamás said, "I think the fire's mostly out already. This guy"—he jerked his thumb at the knight in shining armor—"he got everybody lined up in a bucket brigade. Staci, your Pop, even Mr. Barnes helped in the end, after he got done whining and threatening to sue everybody. Professor Van der Clute straightened him out, all right, told him he owed this knight guy a gold medal for hauling his ass out of the fire. The firemen won't have much left to do when they finally get here."

The sirens grew louder, wailing down Steephill Road.

"Oh, man, I got to get out of here!" cried the knight in shining armor. "I can't let those guys see me in this goofy gear. I *know* them. I'm a volunteer fireman!"

CHAPTER XIII

A World of Glass

After that Timias had againe recured
The favour of Belphebe (as ye heard),
And of her grace did stand againe assured,
To happie blisse he was full high uprear'd,
Nether of envy, nor of chaunge afeard,
Though many foes did him maligne therefore,
And with unjust detraction him did beard;
Yet he himself so well and wisely bore,
That in her soveraine lyking he dwelt evermore.

—*The Faerie Queene*, VI, 5

STACI BOYD STOPPED at their table. She balanced a full lunch tray, a loose-leaf binder, and a pair of pink ballet slippers.

"Is this a private club, or can I sit here, too?"

Phoebe pushed together her own tray and Tamás's to make room for Staci.

"What were you guys talking about?" said Staci. "You had your heads together like you were making big plans."

"Sort of," said Phoebe. "I talked to Althea on the phone last night. She's in Philadelphia, on her tour, you know. She was saying that maybe after she gets back we could go to a recording studio, and Tamás could make some tapes. Althea knows people at the Juilliard. She thinks they would be interested."

"The Juilliard! But, Phoebe... but the *Juilliard*, that's really famous. I mean, like, he could end up famous, too."

"Sure he will," said Phoebe, before Tamás got a chance to say anything stupid.

"You want my dessert?" said Staci, making big eyes at Tamás, as if they'd only just met. Tamás took the dessert.

"I don't see how you can eat that glop," said Phoebe. "I think they make it out of Cool Whip and old bubblegum."

He shrugged. "Probably. There's a lifetime supply stuck under this table."

Phoebe and Staci talked about Drama Club. Staci and Jennifer Gorton were already in it. Phoebe was thinking about joining.

"The thing is, I don't like to be on the spot, performing," said Phoebe. "What I'd really like to try is play *writing*."

She'd been grounded for the last three weeks, since Althea found out from Mrs. Gorton about the skipped tryouts. Althea didn't believe in letting anybody avoid due consequences.

But Althea had also had a talk with Pop. "My parents say I can take a semester off Orchestra, if I feel like I need to. If I want to try out any different electives," Phoebe told Staci. "I haven't really decided yet."

By this time their table had collected Jennifer and Michelle and Andrea, who always followed in wedge formation behind Staci. Andy Polski leaned over from the next table to blow a straw paper at Jennifer. It landed in the mess of pink pudding in front of Tamás. The paper tried to settle down quickly, like the Swamp Thing. But Tamás threw it back anyway. In some ways he was pretty much like other guys.

Phoebe doodled an X with spilled milk on the tabletop. That meant *exit*. It was the secret signal she and Tamás had agreed on for when one of them wanted a private talk.

Tamás gathered up his trash and dumped it on Phoebe's tray. "I better get going," he said. "I've got half a sheet of problems to finish before fifth period."

"Yeah, me too," said Phoebe. "See you later, Staci... Jennifer."

Tamás got rid of the tray. They went out the No Exit door and around behind the gym, where there was a locked shed for storing sports equipment. The side of the shed was painted dark green. It held the warmth of the sun and felt good against Phoebe's back.

"What I wanted to tell you," she said, "is, yesterday I looked in Pop's closet—for that wizard robe, you know? The one with the stars. And it turns out he has this old blue flannel bathrobe, like an Indian blanket, sort of."

"Don't tell me," said Tamás, sliding down onto the ground beside her. "It has stars on it, right?"

"Tamás, I feel like it all never really happened! Like it was a game we made up."

"The Barn Marché really did burn," Tamás pointed out. "Do you think Mr. Barnes will get it fixed up?"

Phoebe shook her head. "The property's for sale. Staci's mother—she sells real estate—she told Staci Mr. Barnes went to live with his sister in Palm Springs. She said his lawyer's handling the sale for him, because Mr. Barnes is a Broken Man."

"Good!" said Tamás. "What else did Staci say?"

"Nothing, really. She didn't even say that to me; I overheard her telling Jennifer Gorton. She was *there,* same as us, but she doesn't act like it was real. Maybe she thinks it's a dream or something. Anyway, she always changes the subject if I try to talk about it."

"What about your parents, haven't they ever said anything? Your mother must've noticed when your pop came home after dark dressed in his bathrobe. Or whatever it was."

"It's more complicated than that. He was sick for so long, and then when he should've been getting better he just kept acting weirder, you know. I mean, she was worried *anyway*. And then sometime that afternoon, while we were down by the river, she went into his study to take him some tea or something, and she couldn't find him. By the time we got home she was practically out of her tree. But Pop started telling about the fire, and... well, you could see right away he was different. Then all of a sudden it was half past eight, and Pop said he was starving and why didn't we go to Wintersham for a pizza? I mean, when was the last time he even noticed what he ate, or *if* he did?"

"But what about you?" Tamás insisted. "Why didn't you ask some questions, find out what they knew?"

"You don't understand how it was. Althea—I mean, she hates pizza, but she looked so *happy*. I didn't want to mess with it, you know? So I didn't say anything. And it's funny, she must've been feeling the same way, because she didn't even mention about talking to Mrs. Gorton until the next day."

"I bet she had plenty to mention about it then."

"About skipping, sure. Not about the other stuff."

"I saw your pop at the college last week," said Tamás. "Actually, he gave me a ride in, to see Professor Bacall."

"Yeah, he told me."

"So is he going back to teaching now?"

"Not till next year," said Phoebe. "Right now he's still working on his book. But he goes to the college all the time to use the library, and at dinner he tells jokes and sees what he eats. The zombie man's all gone."

Tamás slanted up one eyebrow. "My mother says I used to be a good boy, but nowadays I talk back all the time. She thinks I'm turning into an American."

"But she's going to let you go to New York with us, isn't she? To make the tapes?"

"Oh yes," said Tamás. "She went to church and lit candles for my grandfather—her father. She told him I would play the flute in Moscow and make the Russians weep for what they did to him."

Phoebe wanted to take his hand, but she didn't dare, at school, where some kid might see. There were plenty around like those birthday party giants—terminally immature. She kicked Tamás's ankle instead. He took her hand. He was suicidal.

"Don't worry about it," he said, reading her thoughts. "We're tougher than any of them."

She was quiet awhile, feeling the sun on her face; and his shoe bumped against hers. Around the other side of the school building a tractor mower was cutting the grass for the first time that spring. The sweet smell of grass was in the air.

"Listen, Tamás," she said, "what I really need to know is, did all that stuff really happen, or did we make it up?"

"Both," said Tamás. "It really happened *because* we made it up."

"But that's what bothers me," said Phoebe. "I mean, it's not exactly the usual thing, is it, for people to make stuff up like that? It was so real... It was *magic*. What does it mean that we did that? What does it make us?"

"Poets," said Tamás.